MW01200844

THE GENTLE PATRIOT

Georgia Patriots Romance

CAMI CHECKETTS

Birch River
PUBLISHING

COPYRIGHT

CHAPTER ONE

Mack Quinn, offensive lineman for the Georgia Patriots, followed the crowd of his teammates as they surged toward Hyde Metcalf, their wide receiver, to celebrate the winning touchdown pass. A win against Dallas on Christmas Day was great vindication after Dallas had beaten the Patriots out of their spot in the Super Bowl last year. Teammates slapped Hyde on the shoulder and someone hoisted their quarterback, Rigby "the Rocket" Breeland, into the air, but Hyde Metcalf dodged anyone trying to slow him down.

Staying close to his fellow linemen, Mack tried to keep up with Hyde, and blend in with the crowd. Not an easy feat when you were six-eight and over three hundred pounds. Luckily, Mack could move fast, even if his siblings and teammates teased him that he was built like a Mack truck.

He approached the sidelines and watched as Hyde launched himself over the barrier and into the waiting arms of his fiancée,

Lily Udy. Mack's gaze didn't linger on the couple kissing, he searched for the young woman who accompanied Hyde's mom and fiancée to every game. He stopped in his tracks and let out an audible sigh. Sariah Udy.

Somebody ran into him from behind, but he couldn't do more than mutter, "It's okay," to their apology. The woman of his dreams was less than ten feet away from him ... and she had absolutely no clue that he existed. Sariah was cheering, along with her family, as Hyde and Lily kissed and then Hyde started hugging everybody.

Mack had a great family of his own. He'd meet up with them after he showered. He'd bought them a private box last year when he started playing professionally. Usually, a few siblings and his parents were at each home game, sometimes the entire family would show. Today it was his parents, his sister, Navy, and his brother, Colt. Ryder had a game of his own with the Texas Titans tonight, Kaleb was doing a benefit concert in California for Christmas, and Griff was off saving the world somewhere.

He loved his family being here, but he thought it was pretty great that Hyde's family sat on the front row. Maybe he'd move his family's seats next year, if they wanted. The youngest in the family, Mack had never been one to ask much of anybody, especially his family who were much too good to him. He was blessed for sure. If only he could have the blessing of Sariah Udy noticing him. His gaze was still locked on her. She was helping Hyde's mom get her scarf on properly. It was a mild Georgia winter, but the older lady probably chilled easily.

Mack knew far too much about the Metcalf and Udy families. It couldn't really be considered stalking as they'd garnered a lot of media attention last spring when Hyde and Lily had a turbulent love story splashed all over the tabloids. Back then he'd found all the stories interesting about Lily's large family and how her six younger siblings had all fallen in love with Hyde. The first time Mack saw Lily's sister, Sariah, in person the stories went from interesting to fascinating.

It had been the first game of pre-season, August fifth to be exact, and Mack had run on the field with the team, excited for the start of his second year with the Patriots. As he neared his sideline, he'd glanced up at the stands, noticed Sariah, and plowed into the backup quarterback, Tate Campbell. Luckily, he didn't knock Tate to the ground. After Mack apologized, he focused back on Sariah. She was an unreal beauty with olive skin, deep brown eyes, high cheekbones, pouty lips, and long, dark hair. Her thick hair swooped across her forehead, covering the right side of her face and neck, her right eye barely visible through the cloud of hair. The look made her even more exotic and appealing to him.

She'd met his gaze that first day and they simply stared at each other. A silent communication happened between them that he'd never experienced before and for some insane reason he felt like he could see past her beauty to a tender, yet funny woman who always put other's needs before her own. He'd even gone so far as to imagine she could see past his thick muscles, "pretty boy" face—his brothers' words not his—and shyness, to his heart that needed someone like her to understand him.

The communication came to an abrupt halt when someone nudged him and muttered, "The national anthem, dude."

Mack had whirled around to salute the flag. Since that day,

before and after games he was staring at the stands, and quite often she'd be looking his way also. He hadn't dared approach her in the past three months but today was Christmas and he'd decided his gift to himself was to get brave enough to say hello. It was a small step, but he had to start somewhere.

Now, as he waited directly below Sariah, praying she'd glance his way, he started second-guessing himself. Just because he'd fallen hopelessly for her didn't mean she even knew who he was. Maybe all these times he thought she'd been tangling glances with him, she'd truly just been watching the game, or worse, she'd been staring at Tate Campbell or somebody like that who could flirt with a woman like her without their tongue swelling in their mouth.

Sariah finished helping Hyde's mom. The family was still focused on Hyde and Sariah's little brother, Josh, as he exclaimed over the game. Sariah's gaze traveled around the team slowly. Was she searching for him? Mack wanted to yell, "I'm here! Look down." But he didn't. He was the biggest chicken he knew.

Sariah finally seemed to sense him staring at her and her eyes met his. Mack tried to sputter out a hello, but he couldn't have said anything to save even his mama's life.

A slow grin curved Sariah's full lips and her deep brown eyes sparkled at him. She pulled her hair forward on the right side, twisting it in front of her neck. Mack was panting for air worse than when they made him run sprints at practice. He savored every second of the connection, knowing it couldn't last. He'd never gotten this close to her, but he'd watched her after every home game of the season. She'd head up the stairs with her sister and Hyde's mom soon and he'd be left watching her go, like always.

Instead of turning away she stepped right up to the railing, leaned over, and reached her hand down, still giving him that beautiful and inviting smile. Mack's heart leapt. He felt like a loyal knight who might get the opportunity to touch the beautiful princess' hand after winning the tournament.

Usually, Mack was light and fast on his feet, even with his large size. Right now, he lumbered forward, his size fourteen feet felt like blocks of cement, and all he wanted was to get close to her faster.

Finally, he reached the wall and luckily, he was tall enough he didn't have to reach up very far to wrap his hand around her delicate fingers. A zing of awareness and warmth shot through him. His brain tried to keep up with his heart but his heart was singing too loud, *Sariah Udy is holding my hand!*

She smiled down at him. The smile was sweet and welcoming and all the oxygen rushed out of Mack's body. He could face down the most vicious defenders on the field, but he had no clue how to react to holding Sariah's hand and having her smile at him like that.

The roaring crowd around them disappeared as they focused on each other. Mack knew right at that moment—he was in serious like and he had to do something about it. He'd dated different girls throughout high school, college, and the past couple of years women had chased him relentlessly, but he'd never felt a connection like this. This had to be the right woman for him.

"Hi," she said softly.

"Hi," Mack dumbly repeated. He squeezed her hand, he hoped gently, and searched his muddled brain for something poetic to say. His brother, Kaleb, was a professional country singer and had all manner of beautiful things to say or sing. His brother, Colt, was a professional woman-magnet and had trained Mack relentlessly on how to give a woman a smoldering look or say the right phrase to draw her in.

Mack prayed for inspiration and finally muttered, "Hi, pretty girl."

His face flamed red. What had he just said? He probably sounded like a creeper or something. That line had worked on his older brothers' girlfriends when Mack was eight and cute. Now he was twenty-five and hopefully there was nothing cute about him.

Sariah let out a soft chuckle and then tugged her hand free, waved quickly to him, and hurried to her family. Mack watched them all walk away. Her dad gave him a backwards, concerned glance, but Sariah didn't turn around or acknowledge him again.

Mack felt like he'd been slugged in the abdomen by his brother, Griff, the ex-navy SEAL who could take down any man. His big chance and he'd messed it all up. *Hi, pretty girl?* Sheesh, he was an idiot.

Most of the partying in the stadium had calmed and people were flowing out of the stands. A lot of his teammates were gone to the locker room. He trudged that direction. As he entered the double doors, he smiled at the party that was going on—singing, joking, back-slapping. He walked through, receiving and handing out congrats and inflated praise.

Then he saw Hyde and his footsteps faltered. Did he dare ask for Sariah's number? How did you tell a guy his future sister-in-law was destined to love you? No way. Too gutsy.

He wussed out and went to his own locker. He took his time showering and chatting with teammates. He headed out of the locker room, ready to find his family and fly to Ryder's game tonight then on to Newport, Rhode Island, for a long-awaited family Christmas party tomorrow morning. He realized he was walking side by side with none other than Hyde Metcalf. It was a sign and he couldn't ignore it.

"Hey, man." He tilted his chin up. "Great game."

"Thanks." Hyde clapped him on the shoulder. "We couldn't have done it without you. You're a beast out there."

"Thanks." It was so like Hyde to shift the praise and not get caught up on himself. They were approaching the locker room door and Mack knew it was now or never. He put his hand on Hyde's forearm and stopped walking. Hyde turned to him with a questioning glance. Mack shoved a hand through his hair. "Hey, um, your sister-in-law ... Sariah?"

"Yeah?" Hyde's glance wasn't as friendly now. Suspicious, wary, concerned.

"You couldn't, um, give me her number?" Why was everything coming out as a question? He was a Quinn. His brothers, sister, and mama would all disown him if they found out about his wimpy thoughts and actions tonight.

Hyde looked him over. "I can't just give out Sariah's number."

"Oh." Disappointment stabbed him. "Could you see if she wants my number?"

"How do you know Sariah?"

"I ... I don't. But she touched my hand tonight." It was official. He was the most pathetic man in the world and he was revealing it all to Hyde Metcalf. He was going to get laughed off the field at their next practice.

Hyde's eyebrows arched. "I'm sorry, Mack. You seem like a nice guy, but I don't know you that well, and Sariah is ... special to all of us. An angel really, with a funny sense of humor." Hyde smiled briefly.

Mack knew that was true simply from looking at her. Pure goodness, light, and humor radiated from her.

"She lives in Denver," Hyde continued. "So, it really wouldn't work. Sorry, man." With that he pushed through the locker room door and was gone.

Mack sat there staring at the door until some other players came up behind him and he walked woodenly through to avoid explaining why he hadn't moved—he'd just had all his hopes doused in fire retardant and they would never burn bright again.

CHAPTER TWO

Sariah Udy's job of being Hyde's mom's companion was absolutely perfect for her. She was able to drive into Denver every weekday for her schooling as a massage therapist and nights and weekends she spent time with Teresa. Quite often Hyde and Lily or other members of her family would be with them. She also loved Teresa's neighbor and spicy friend, Allie. It was a great arrangement, made even better by the fact that they flew to most Patriot games and she got the opportunity to watch Mack Quinn play football.

Mack Quinn. She loved to simply watch the man move. He was massive and not one spare inch of him was fat. Most people hardly noticed what the offensive line did at a football game. Sariah couldn't pull her eyes off the offensive line. In her mind, Mack was poetry in motion and he never missed a block or other assignment.

Then there were the times before and after games when he met her gaze, his blue eyes warm and completely focused on her. She lived for those moments. On Christmas Day he'd come over to the sidelines and he'd not only wrapped his hand around hers he'd said, "Hi, pretty girl". It was the most beautiful moment of her life.

Sariah knew nothing could come of her obsession. Someone with her deformity could never be with someone perfect, rich, and famous like Mack Quinn. She'd learned that lesson all too well from her high school boyfriend. The fact that she'd never do more than stare at Mack hurt, but she didn't let herself dwell on it. She'd made a happy life for herself by simply putting a smile on her face each day and making it a great day. Falling in that campfire at five-years-old may have deformed her right ear and left her with horrific-looking scar tissue on her neck, shoulder, and upper arm, but it couldn't take her down.

Today was the last playoff game before the Super Bowl. The entire family was in Los Angeles, California, cheering for Hyde. He and Lily's dream wedding was going to happen in March, after the season ended, and Sariah couldn't be happier for them. If only she could have a dream one day, a dream like Mack Quinn. He seemed so kind, despite his strength. He looked just like Thor to her, a bigger and more approachable Thor. Sadly, he wasn't attainable for her. His family were all superstars—a country singer, two professional football players, a fitness guru, a highly-decorated ex-Navy SEAL, and a media darling. The media would destroy Mack if he dated someone with Sariah's deformity. She knew that from personal experience. It had been hard enough on Lily and Hyde to overcome the media's scrutiny of the discrepancy in their financial stations. It would be even worse for her. As if a man like Mack could look past her mottled skin.

She touched her neck self-consciously, making sure the hair covered her scars, even as she rolled her eyes at herself. It was silly to even speculate. Since Christmas Day, almost a month ago, when Mack had actually approached her, stolen her breath away when he wrapped his strong hand around hers, and called her "pretty girl", he hadn't made any other move. He still caught her gaze before or after games but he kept his distance. She tucked her hair tighter against the right side of her face and around her neck. Had he seen her puckered skin when he got close? He hadn't recoiled in disgust so she didn't think so. Something was keeping him away from her. Maybe it was because she'd only been capable of saying hi when confronted with his perfect smile up close and personal.

Focusing on the game, she waited for even a simple glance. The smells of pizza, popcorn, and cotton candy floated around her. She loved football and the atmosphere. Mack played brilliantly and every time the offense ran off the field, she studied him and she could've sworn he glanced her direction a few times, but she could just be imagining it. The game ended with Georgia beating Washington 21 to 14. She cheered along with everybody and she waited and watched for Mack to look her way. Hyde ran over to them but he didn't launch himself over the barrier like he had on Christmas. Lily bent over and he squeezed her hands and they talked excitedly.

Teresa watched them with a satisfied smile on her face. The future in-law relationship had a rocky start last spring, but almost a year later and everybody adored each other. Sariah loved Hyde and Teresa and really appreciated how good they were to her. Five more months and she'd be a licensed massage therapist. Teresa and Hyde had both expressed that they hoped she'd stay in the apartment above the garage at Teresa's Golden, Colorado house as long as she wanted. The apartment was bigger than her family home in Georgetown, Colorado and nicer than any place she'd been in. She couldn't see any reason not to continue the arrangement.

Her eyes strayed from her happy sister to find Mack Quinn. He was in a cluster of players about thirty feet away from her. He was chatting with all of them but his gaze was pinned on Sariah. She tucked her hair tighter to her face and neck. It was a nervous gesture she really needed to quit, but she wanted this man to get to know her before he was repulsed by her scars and ran away. She was so lame. He couldn't run away when he'd never run to her.

Mack excused himself from the group and walked her direction. Her heart thudded quicker and quicker. Was he finally going to approach her again? It was what she'd been dreaming of. This time she had to be braver than to just offer her hand and say hi. How old-fashioned was that? Guaranteed, Mack Quinn had gorgeous women pushing themselves at him every day and here she offered her hand to him? No matter how dumb it may have been, she'd re-lived the feel of his hand surrounding hers and loved each replay.

He kept coming, his gaze trained on her. Her legs were weak and she edged closer to the barrier in front of her and leaned against it. With every footstep that brought him closer, her heart seemed to be shouting, Mack, Mack, Mack. His blue eyes were bluer than the Colorado sky in the summertime, and even though his blond curls were matted to his head from his helmet, he looked unreal handsome. She could've sworn that he looked nervous. That couldn't be. He was an enigma and she was a dirt-poor girl from nowhere.

His steps slowed as he approached her and his gaze darted to Hyde and Lily. Sariah focused on them also but they were so full of each other they wouldn't have noticed if a bomb dropped in the stadium. The rest of her family was also focused on Hyde and Lily. Teresa was staring at Mack though, and she lifted a perfectly-formed eyebrow at Sariah. Sariah smiled at her before refocusing on Mack. He was right below her now, just like he'd been on Christmas Day.

She leaned over the barrier but didn't put her hand out. This time she was going to try to at least talk to him. "You pummeled them," she said.

"We do our best." He pushed a hand through his hair. His voice was low and appealing but on the quiet side. She wanted to know so much about him. She wanted to listen to him talk for hours.

"It's an impressive best."

He smiled. "Gotta protect your brother-in-law."

"Aw, that's sweet. He hasn't won the role of brother-in-law yet, but he keeps hoping." She grinned at Hyde, Lily, and Teresa, who were all watching them now, along with her parents and siblings. Embarrassment filtered in. Would her family and Hyde's be thinking, *what is sweet little Sariah doing talking to the big, bad football player? She could never hope to date someone like him.*

"We'll see if he gets my stamp of approval before March." She tried to act confident and not reveal to Mack yet how pathetic she was.

Mack chuckled softly and it was the most glorious sound. Sariah wanted to help him make that sound every day of his life. Whew, she was racing ahead of herself.

The rest of her family and Teresa were looking at the two of them with interested smiles. Well, except for her dad, but he was crazy overprotective of her since her publicized heartbreak and humiliation almost four years ago. Hyde looked ... ticked. She tried to remember if she'd ever seen Hyde ticked. Even last year when Lily had been livid with him when she blamed him for Josh and Caleb's accident and she'd slapped him across the face at the hospital, he'd responded humbly. Did he not appreciate Sariah teasing him? That made no sense, she always teased Hyde. He was the big brother she'd never had. She had plenty of younger brothers and they were great, but a fun-loving, bantering, and slightly overprotective big brother was amazing.

Her brow wrinkled and she tugged at her hair. Had she said something wrong? Had she exposed her scars? She turned her right side slightly away from Mack just to make sure. Normally she would escape the situation, but this might be her one and only chance to talk to Mack Quinn. She had to be bold and stay in it. Then she could live on the memories of the interaction for a long, long time.

"Hyde's a good man, I'm sure he'll get that stamp," Mack said in his low, melodious tone.

Sariah absolutely loved Mack's brother Kaleb's, country music.

She felt like Mack's voice was very similar to his brother. Wouldn't it be glorious if she could talk him into singing?

Instead of smiling at the interaction and Mack's compliment, Hyde released Lily's hands and gestured with his chin toward the locker room. "Let's go," he said shortly to Mack.

Mack studied him briefly, as if debating if he should tackle him or obey him. Hyde folded his arms across his chest and arched an eyebrow. Mack focused back on Sariah. "It was nice to see you," he said.

"It was lovely to be seen." She winked boldly at him. She hadn't been bold with a man in years, but this might be the only chance she had to talk to him. She begged him with her eyes to ask for her number, or if she wanted to go for milkshakes after the game or something. Okay, maybe milkshakes after the game was a high school thing and would reveal she hadn't dated since close to high school age, but she desperately wanted to extend their time together.

Mack gifted her with his melodious chuckle then he tossed an imperious glare at Hyde and strode past him to the locker room. Hyde gave them all a forced smile. "I'll see you in a bit," he muttered before storming after Mack.

"What was that all about?" Lily murmured.

"I'm as clueless as a man at a makeup counter," Sariah said.

The family all laughed like they always did at her lame jokes then Josh and Caleb started recounting every play that Hyde had made today. Sariah watched Mack disappear into the tunnel that led to the locker room, Hyde hot on his heels. It was almost as if Hyde didn't want Mack talking to her.

Sariah thought through and savored each word and smile. Although she didn't expect anything to come of it, she knew someone as perfect as Mack Quinn could never be with her, but she still wanted to talk to Mack more.

M ack rarely got upset, even when he'd been teased about a speech impediment as a child. He'd shut down and stopped talking, but he didn't remember being mad. When he'd been kidnapped last spring as a ploy by a criminal to capture his new sister-in-law, Jasmine, he'd been uncomfortable, upset, and concerned but not outright angry. Right now, he was ticked. Hyde Metcalf had no reason to shut him down when he was finally having a conversation with Sariah. He'd respected Hyde over the past month and not approached Sariah, but he knew, *knew* that she stared at him throughout each game he played, and he could not get her out of his head. He'd had to at least *try* to have a decent conversation with her. Now he had and he wanted more.

He made it into the tunnel leading to the locker room, made sure there were no press anywhere, and whirled to face Hyde. Hyde came up short and glared at him. "I warned you to stay away from her."

"No." Mack shook his head and folded his arms across his chest. A lesser man would've cowered at the sight of his cut and massive biceps. Hyde didn't flinch. "You told me she was a special angel to all of you and that she lived in Denver. You didn't demand I stay away."

"You're right." Hyde pushed a hand through his hair. "I'm sorry, Mack, I respect you and I like you, but I need to ask you to stay away from Sariah."

"Why?" he demanded. "She's an adult. She can make her own choices."

"She can," Hyde agreed. "And believe me this has nothing to do with you personally, but your family is well-known and Sariah just can't be exposed to the media like that. She's not ready for that emotionally. It would tear her apart."

"Why?" Mack asked again.

Hyde blew out a breath. "It's her story to tell, but please just listen to me. She's been ... injured in so many ways and she's like the little sister I never had. I have to protect her."

Mack hated, hated the thought of Sariah being injured. Some man had hurt her, or was it something else? He respected that Hyde wouldn't share her secrets but how was Mack to find out those secrets from Sariah if Hyde wouldn't condone him being near her? He tried to soften his stance, releasing his clenched arms and rolling his shoulders back.

"I would never hurt her," he said softly.

Hyde looked him over. The moments stretched on too long and Mack thought he should put up a better argument. This woman was all he'd ever dreamed of and he needed the chance to get to know her.

"I'm not saying you'd try to hurt her, but I just can't take the risk that you, or everything you would bring with you, wouldn't inadvertently hurt her. You don't understand Sariah. How sweet she is. What she's gone through." He shook his head. "If you respect me at all, please stay away from her."

Hyde strode around him and disappeared into the locker room. Mack called himself all kinds of names for not going after the guy and begging him, or pinning him down until he conceded. The problem was he did respect Hyde, and even though he didn't know Sariah, he cared for her far too much to risk hurting her. Yet his mind whirled with ways to get around Hyde's request and somehow talk to Sariah. The devotion he already felt to her meant he couldn't give up, without her being the one to tell him to stay away.

CHAPTER THREE

Sariah looked around in awe at the owner of the Patriots' mansion. It looked like something straight out of *Gone with the Wind* only modernized and much, much bigger. The three-story mansion had the classic columns of a plantation home with a huge wrap-around porch encompassing the first and second levels. Sariah fancied herself sitting on one of the rocking chairs on the second story overlooking the tree-lined driveway and sweeping lawns and waiting for her love to ride up on horseback. The man she envisioned was large and had blond curls and bright blue eyes. She needed to stop her Mack Quinn fantasies. Mack hadn't tried to approach her at the Super Bowl, not since the weird way Hyde pulled him away when he was talking to Sariah at the playoff game in California. She wanted to ask Hyde about it but he'd been understandably busy and there hadn't been a conducive moment.

The party tonight was to celebrate the Patriots' win over San

Francisco. They were champions this year and Sariah's youngest brother Josh couldn't stop talking about it. He was adorable. Sariah had been invited to this party to accompany Teresa. She assumed it was because Hyde and Lily would be busy mingling and everyone wanted to make sure Teresa didn't wander off or say something she shouldn't. The lovely lady had been diagnosed with early-onset Alzheimer's last year and she was doing well, but sometimes she got forgetful or confused.

Teresa and Sariah wandered around the vast ballroom together, trying some of the food, talking, and mostly people-watching. There were a lot of well-known celebrities, in addition to all the football players who were famous in their own right. Sariah made sure her hair was in place. Self-conscious didn't begin to describe how she felt in this situation. These were the shiny, happy people and she didn't fit. Lily not only fit, she rose above others around her because of her kindness, natural beauty, and spunk. Sariah was so proud of her sister, and wished she could hide behind her.

The owner of the Patriots, Bucky Buchanan, dominated the scene. Sariah had heard he was a storyteller and she could see crowds gathered around him as his boisterous voice carried from twenty feet away.

Her eyes kept wandering as she prayed that Mack Quinn would be here. All the players should be here, so why not him?

Teresa tensed beside her and Sariah immediately refocused. "Teresa? Are you all right?"

Teresa nodded but her breath was coming too fast for Sariah's liking. Sariah took one of her hands and started kneading it gently between both of her own. Any kind of massage calmed Teresa down but Sariah didn't think it was a great idea to grab her employer's shoulders and start working on relaxation techniques at this upscale party.

"I'm fine, sweetie," Teresa murmured. "Look."

Sariah followed Teresa's gaze and noticed the owner, Bucky, striding toward them. He wasn't exactly handsome but he had a commanding presence with a well-worn face and a cowboy look that reminded Sariah of John Wayne. People tried to waylay him and he would graciously shake their hands and say a few words with him but didn't stop for long. He was obviously focused on reaching Teresa. His eyes were a deep blue and they twinkled as he approached Sariah and Teresa. His entourage didn't follow him, but many eyes in the room were watching his progress.

He extended both hands to Teresa. "Teresa Metcalf, as I live and breathe," his Southern accent was charming and Sariah noticed Teresa was blushing prettily. "How do you become more beautiful every time I see you?"

Teresa pulled her hand free of Sariah's grasp and clasped his hands. "You old charmer. I don't believe a word of your flattery."

Sariah hid a laugh. These two were flirting. In front of the crowd. She looked around for Hyde and Lily and saw them clear across the ballroom. They weren't aware Bucky was hitting on Teresa yet. Teresa's divorce from Hyde's dad, who deserted them both a year ago, had only been finalized last month. Sariah had never seen Teresa so much as glance at a man her age.

"You know I couldn't tell a lie if someone hogtied me and branded me for it," Bucky said. "Your beauty is unsurpassed and

I'm pleased as a good shot of whiskey that you've graced my home with your lovely face."

"You stop it." Teresa pulled one hand and waved it in front of her face. "You'll make me blush."

"You're already blushing, darlin'." He winked at her then finally released her hands and offered his hand to Sariah. "Sariah Hyde? It's a pleasure to make your acquaintance, little lady."

Sariah shook his hand, surprised he knew who she was, but she and Lily did look quite a bit alike. "You even talk like John Wayne."

He joined in her laughter, not appearing the least bit put out. "But I'm much more charming and wealthy, right?" He arched an eyebrow as if daring her to refuse him.

"Charming as a lion, I'm sure."

"Teresa thinks I'm charming." He turned his attention back to her. "Now that I've got you here, I have to show you my gardens." He extended his elbow to her then glanced at Sariah. "You don't mind, do you?"

Sariah shook her head, though it worried her to not be close to Teresa. Would Hyde care? Who would Sariah talk to in this crowd?

Teresa gave Sariah a happy grin as she and Bucky started across the ballroom toward a balcony door. It was probably a great boost for Teresa to feel pretty and desirable after what her ex-husband had put her through, but Sariah worried. What if Teresa got confused or said something that offended Bucky, who was basically Hyde's boss?

They disappeared out the open door and Sariah hurried to where Hyde and Lily were chatting with Rigby Breeland and his wife. Hyde saw her coming and he must've seen the concern on her face because he excused himself and hurried to meet her. "Are you okay?"

"I'm fine," she said. "But your mom went on a stroll with Bucky Buchanan out to his gardens."

Hyde's shoulders lowered and he smiled. "Bucky's a good guy and he knows everything about my mom. He'll be kind to her."

"Okay. I just feel so responsible for her."

"Thanks, Sariah."

"I'll go sit outside and keep an eye out," Sariah said.

"Thanks." He turned back to Lily and the Breelands, who were watching both of them.

Sariah smiled at her sister so Lily would know she was fine. Both Hyde and Lily had been worried about her coming tonight, knowing she didn't like attention and was happier doing her massage therapy or working in the garden with Teresa and Allie. The thing she hadn't told them was she wanted to come, hoping to see Mack Quinn.

She hurried toward the door Bucky and Teresa had disappeared out of and searched the property. The pool area was well-lit and landscaped with waterfalls, decorative pools, and a couple of hot tubs. Sariah strode down the descending patios, past the pools, and saw the beautiful flower gardens. The lights in the garden were softer but Sariah could still see several couples strolling along the lit paths that were filled with some spring flowers in bloom and others still budding, flowering bushes, and trees. The darkness beyond looked to be a thick forest. It smelled fresh out here, similar to the Colorado mountains that she loved so much. She wished she could see it all in the daylight.

Walking slowly to the main path, she sank into a comfy, padded bench and waited for Teresa and Bucky to appear again. She hoped they wouldn't think she was stalking them but the night air was mild and she'd rather be alone in this garden than hiding in a crowd full of people. Especially if Mack wasn't coming tonight.

M ack arrived at the Super Bowl celebration party later than he'd wanted. Atlanta traffic could be horrible sometimes and he'd been caught in a traffic jam heading out to Marietta. When he arrived, he greeted fellow players but his eyes searched the spacious ballroom for Hyde Metcalf. He hoped Lily and maybe even Sariah would be here tonight. Since Hyde had rebuffed him from pursuing Sariah, for the second time, he'd stewed about what to do. He'd decided to try to get Sariah's sister, Lily, alone and get her take on the situation. Maybe he could soften her and get her approval and maybe even Sariah's phone number.

As his eyes finally found Hyde, his stomach hopped when he realized Hyde wasn't talking to Lily but to Sariah. Her long, dark hair swooped over her right shoulder, covering her neck. Her knee-length pale blue gown fit her beautiful shape perfectly. It was an interesting dress with a high neckline, long sleeves, and no back or chest exposed. It made Mack appreciate Sariah all the more. Her beauty was unequaled and she didn't need to be showing off skin to anyone.

Sariah strode away from Hyde and out a patio door. Hyde returned to Lily's side, talking to the Rocket and his wife.

Mack felt like a sneaky teenager, but he knew this was his first and maybe only opportunity. He would be very cautious not to make Sariah uncomfortable, but he needed to know if he had any chance with her. He respected Hyde, but still felt Sariah was an adult who should be able to decide who she associated with.

Staying on the outskirts of the ballroom, he approached the exterior patio door from a different direction, keeping an eye on Hyde and Lily. Neither of them glanced his way.

As he exited the ballroom, he found himself on the back patio. He searched around the pool area and couldn't see Sariah anywhere. Walking slowly, he finally saw her at the entrance to the main garden path. She sat on a bench, facing the opening of the path. He couldn't see her face clearly but he would recognize her thick, dark hair and perfect shape anywhere.

Mack increased his pace, his breath coming quicker in anticipation. If Sariah waiting for him on a garden bench wasn't a sign from above that she should be in his life, he didn't know what was.

CHAPTER FOUR

Sariah didn't mind waiting for Teresa and Bucky. Hushed conversations from the garden floated to her, along with some giggles and laughs. Obviously, more couples than Teresa and Bucky were enjoying a stroll, or more. It made Sariah smile. If only she could be one of those couples, with Mack. She shook her head. He hadn't come to the party. She'd pinned all her hopes of truly connecting with the man she'd been staring at all season on this party. It felt like her last chance. If she didn't see Mack tonight, she might not see him until next fall. The offseason for the players had officially started. Google had informed her that Mack had a condo in Atlanta and a home near his parent's place in Newport, Rhode Island. She didn't have any way to contact him. Maybe she could follow him on Instagram, comment on his every post, and hope he'd contact her. That was dumb. He surely had someone hired to manage all his social media, and protect him from star-crazed women like her.

Footsteps approached. Fear filled her and the horrid memories resurfaced of being held underwater until she wanted to die. She shook that off, stood quickly, and whirled to face the threat head-on.

Mack Quinn strode determinedly toward her. All fears disappeared. He looked magnificent in a tailored tux that made him look like a buff international spy instead of a football player.

Sariah's breath caught in her throat. He stopped a couple of feet away, as if worried he would overpower her or frighten her. A slow smile grew on his handsome face. "Hi, pretty girl," he said softly.

Sariah hid a laugh and returned his smile, happiness filling her. "Is that your standard line for every girl?"

Mack shook his head. "You're the only girl I've ever said it to."

Sariah wanted to rush into his arms, but that would be insane and much, much too pushy. "Come on, I can't believe that. I have social media. I know you date a lot of pretty girls."

"I've never dated anyone as beautiful as you." Mack's blue gaze seemed to deepen and he took a couple steps closer to her, close enough she could smell his soft cologne—sandalwood and lavender. It fit him, tough but kind. "I'd better fire my social media people if they're making me look like a player."

Sariah tilted her head back so she could hold his gaze, tucking her hair against her neck just to make sure. "You're even bigger than I thought."

He smiled at that but then he sobered quickly. "Sariah," her name on his lips made her knees quiver. "Did a man hurt you?"

Sariah backed up a step, but ran into the bench and almost fell down onto it. Mack reached out and steadied her with his hand. His palm wrapped around her waist and she felt small and desirable under his touch. But why would he ask something like that? Did he know about Tyler? All the horrible memories resurfaced and she remembered why it wasn't smart to fall for someone high-profile like Mack, but how could she resist him? His blue eyes were tugging her in and his large frame shouted protection to her. There was nothing to fear from Mack. All she wanted was to forget Tyler ever hurt her and to lean in closer to Mack.

Bravely, she did lean closer. It was obvious he was waiting for an answer to his question, but his grip on her waist tightened and he bent toward her. Breathing became difficult as she focused on his handsome face and the depth in his blue eyes. He wanted to be with her, but he was very concerned about who had hurt her in her past. She didn't want to think about her past right now. She wanted to lift up onto her tiptoes and wrap her arms around his broad shoulders.

Voices approached and she tore her eyes from Mack's handsome face to see who was emerging from the garden. Horribly for her, it was Teresa and Bucky.

"Mack Quinn," Bucky's loud voice sang out. He stuck out his hand. "There's my favorite offensive lineman."

Mack chuckled, released his grip on Sariah's waist and shook Bucky's hand. "Nice to see you, sir."

"It's a great night, Mack. We'd better head in, they're going to be doing some sort of awards and singing your praises I'm sure." He winked at Teresa and grinned at Sariah. "Can we escort you lovely ladies inside?"

Teresa shook her head. "We'll enjoy the night air for a bit longer. You go on in."

Bucky nodded. "I wish I could extend our time, but duty calls."

"Of course," Teresa murmured. "Thank you for the stroll."

"My pleasure. I hope to see you again soon." He tipped his nonexistent hat to her and turned, slapping Mack's shoulder. "Ah, offensive linemen are the best. What are you, three hundred pounds?"

"About that," Mack murmured. He gave Sariah one last searching glance but fell in to step with Bucky and headed into the house.

Sariah didn't move, and neither did Teresa, until the men disappeared. Finally, Teresa let out a soft sigh. "Well, sweet Sariah. Do you want to share any secrets with me?"

Sariah swallowed hard. "Sadly, there's nothing to share. How about you?"

Teresa smiled. "Oh, there's a lot to share, but I suspect Bucky Buchanan is just a charmer and nothing will come of our stroll. Do you want to head in for awards?"

Sariah wanted to sit here and wait for Mack to reappear but she knew that probably wasn't happening. "We'd better. I'm sure Hyde will get something."

"Ah, my boy. I'm sure you're right." They walked slowly toward the brightly lit house. Sariah felt depressed and she knew she had no right to. Every interaction with Mack ended much sooner than she wanted it to. If she didn't get another chance to talk to him tonight, she feared their chances had run out.

———

Mack liked Bucky. He was a great owner and a great guy, but him interrupting when Sariah had been leaning in ... curse his boss from here to the South Pole. He cheered along with everyone through the awards ceremony. It was an amazing accomplishment as a team to win the Super Bowl and he was proud to be part of it, but he just wanted more time alone with Sariah.

After the ceremony he talked with different teammates, sponsors, coaches, and some celebrities. His recently-traded fellow lineman and college buddy, Miles Moore, brought a beautiful redhead over to their circle after they finished eating platefuls of the buffet-style dinner. Miles and the redhead could be siblings, except he was twice her size.

Mack smiled at the woman, but his gaze was searching for Sariah as it had been all night. He hadn't seen her or Hyde for a while and was worried they'd left.

"Mack." Miles grinned at him. "I come bearing gifts."

The redhead laughed and rolled her eyes at him. "I'm not a gift, you silly boy." She put her hand out. She looked beautiful in a fitted, off-the-shoulder black dress, but Mack only had eyes for one woman. "Scarlett Lily," she introduced herself.

"Oh." Mack nodded, shaking her hand. "I should've recognized you." He'd only seen a few of her movies, but you'd have to be living in a tent in the South Pole to not know who Scarlett Lily was.

"It's all right. I came tonight hoping to meet you."

Mack's eyebrows lifted. Why would Scarlett Lily want to meet him? She was older than him, extremely famous, and could have any man she wanted. He only wanted Sariah so he hoped this wasn't about Scarlett looking for a date.

She swirled the liquid in her drink and stared at him for a few beats before saying, "I knew your brother in college."

"Which one?" He had a lot of brothers people claimed to know, but he didn't think Scarlett Lily needed the Quinn name to social climb. At least she wasn't after Mack. A lot of women wanted to date a "hot giant", their words not his. It made him uncomfortable. Scarlett seemed really nice, nothing like the cleat chasers.

"Griff," she said.

"You went to USC?" Mack asked to be polite. He noticed his buddies gaping at him as if he were on the movie screen. Talking to Scarlett Lily didn't intimidate or impress him. She was a beautiful woman and he liked her movies, but he really wanted to find Sariah before she disappeared.

"Yeah. Griff and I ... dated." Her smile was warm but there was something in her clear, green eyes that told him Griff had hurt her.

"I'm sorry," he said.

She gave a throaty chuckle and Mack thought she was a brave

lady who didn't need his sympathy, but maybe she needed his brother. He'd have to ask Navy about it. Instead of taking his apology for what it was, *I'm sorry my brother hurt you*. Scarlett turned it to sarcasm and something to laugh about, *I'm sorry you dated the jerk.*

"Griff's a good man." She smiled and her eyes got a faraway look in them. "Always the strong, silent type, unless I tickled him."

Mack's eyebrows lifted. She'd tickled Griff, and lived to tell about it. Scarlett was indeed as brave as the characters she portrayed. "If you thought he was quiet in college you should see him since he retired from the SEALs."

Her smile dropped away. "He made that a little difficult."

"Griff makes most things difficult," he muttered.

Now Scarlett's eyebrows were the ones lifting.

"I love my brother," Mack said. "He is a great man. It's just ..." He didn't know how much he should share but something in her eyes made him feel he could trust her and possibly ease her suffering a little bit. "Griff endures alone and he thinks he does it to protect others—people like me and you."

"You're a wise man," Scarlett said. She moved closer, went onto tiptoes, and kissed his jaw. He thought she'd probably meant to kiss his cheek but he was too tall for her to reach. Her kiss was soft and kind, something a sister or friend would do. Staying close she whispered in his ear, "Tell Griff I asked about him, will you?"

Mack nodded. She gave him one last smile that didn't reach her eyes, and sauntered away to greet some other players, congratulating them on the Super Bowl win. Mack watched her go, wondering at the story between her and Griff and feeling badly for her. It had been common knowledge that she'd been dating the famous hockey player, Josh Porter, last fall. He'd dumped her at Christmas for Callum Hawk's new sister-in-law, Hannah Hall. The press had made a huge deal about it, but somehow Mack didn't think Scarlett had been as invested in Josh as everyone seemed to think. It was obvious to Mack that she cared for his brother. He'd pass her message on, though he doubted Griff would do anything about it. Mack worried Griff, Colt, and Navy would all grow old alone. Griff was too hard, Colt was too much of a player, and Navy was too invested in her career.

Mack had no desire to be alone. He focused on searching for Sariah. The party was starting to thin out and he worried she'd left. If she had, how was he going to find her again? Hyde's request that he stay away from Sariah was so faded he could hardly remember how Hyde had phrased it. Especially when Mack had the remembrance of her waist in his palm and her dark eyes focused on him as she leaned closer in that garden.

CHAPTER FIVE

Sariah wanted to talk to Mack before they left, but the room was crowded throughout the awards and dinner and she, Lily, Hyde, and Teresa stayed close together. She didn't want to just disappear and she didn't want to have to explain her obsession with someone she barely knew.

It was obvious Teresa was tired and some of the party-goers were starting to head out. Hyde said he'd go get his Lexus from the valet. Sariah leaned close to Lily after he left and whispered, "I need to go say goodbye to someone, can you take Teresa to meet Hyde and I'll be right there?"

"Sure." Lily winked. "As long as I get to hear all about this 'someone' back at the hotel." Lily still lived and worked in Golden at the gym where she and Hyde had met. After she and Hyde married, she would relocate to Atlanta. Sariah knew the long-distance relationship hadn't been easy but they were very in love and a solid couple.

Sariah nodded quickly, nervous. She'd only have a minute as she didn't want them waiting for her and wearing out Teresa even more. It had been an exciting night for Teresa between her proud Mom moments with the awards Hyde received and the flirtations that didn't stop from Bucky.

She hurried toward the spot she'd seen Mack talking with a group of players and stopped in her tracks. Mack was leaning in close to a beautiful redhead, speaking intently to her. The woman kissed his jaw and then whispered in his ear. As she pulled back, Sariah recognized her. Scarlett Lily. The famous and beautiful action movie actress.

Mack's eyes followed Scarlett as she walked away in an off-the shoulder black dress that was flattering and alluring. Her skin was smooth, deeper-toned than most redheads Sariah had seen. The thought of Mack gazing at, and possibly touching that lovely skin made Sariah's stomach churn. The truth she'd ignored while talking to Mack in the garden hit her again. She could never be in the same class as Scarlett Lily, or any of the wives or girlfriends of these players. She could never be with someone like the glorious Mack Quinn.

Pulling her hair tighter around her burn marks, Sariah spun on her heel and hurried to meet her sister. Tears stung at her eyes, which was ridiculous. She hardly knew Mack and had no rights to him because of a couple of silly interactions. She was immature and had no clue how relationships with the opposite sex worked. Obviously, she'd been smart to keep her distance from men after Tyler destroyed her emotionally and his girlfriend, Denise, hurt her physically. This just reaffirmed it.

Lily and Teresa were waiting for her in the entry. Lily pumped her eyebrows but Sariah shook her head and looked away. She'd be in for a grilling later, but right now she just wanted to make sure she didn't burst into tears.

CHAPTER SIX

Mack lost all decorum as he searched every spot in the mansion, where the public were welcome to roam, to find Sariah. He'd tried to play it cool earlier but now he was desperate. Finally, he conceded that she'd left and he made the rounds with a heavy feeling inside. He said goodbye to teammates and coaches and finally met Bucky close to the door.

"Thank you, sir, for everything."

Bucky shook his hand vigorously. "Thank you, son. It's been a great couple seasons with you on board." He released his hand but pinned him with a gaze. "Beautiful young lady I saw you with."

"Yes, sir, she is."

"Anything happening there?"

"Unfortunately, not." He forced a smile.

Bucky threw back his head and laughed. "Ah, us poor men. You're a good one, son." He slapped him on the shoulder and moved on to the next person waiting to say goodbye.

Mack's feet were too big for his body as he trudged out the front door and off the porch, handing his ticket to the valet. They finally brought his Range Rover to him and he tipped the valet and then scrunched himself inside, obviously, the valet had to move the seat forward to be able to drive it. Pushing the programmed seat button, Mack relaxed as the seat pushed back and he could stretch out his legs.

Puttering down the tree-lined drive, he debated what he could do, if anything. Calling Hyde wasn't going to get him anywhere. He shook his head, frustrated. Sariah. She'd been right there, and he'd lost her again.

He thought through the night and remembered the conversation with Scarlett. He needed to try to contact Griff and give him Scarlett's message. Sometimes Griff went off the grid and the family couldn't contact him, but he always got back to Mack later. He had told Scarlett the truth, his brother was a great man who did what he did to protect others.

Wait a minute. Griff! His brother could find information no person should be able to find. He pushed the button on his steering wheel and asked to call Griff Quinn.

A few rings later and his brother answered, "Mack." Griff was never warm with anyone, but Mack knew he was a little softer for him. The entire family was. He appreciated their devotion to him, and tried hard never to take advantage of it. Tonight, he might change that.

"Hey, bro. You home?" Home for Griff was Sutton Smith's sprawling mansion in southern California. Griff had plenty of money, but seemed to have no desire to have his own place or settle down. He lived to protect innocent people and put himself in danger.

"Belize."

"Oh." Mack used to ask what Griff was up to, try to have a normal conversation with his brother. He learned quickly Griff wasn't interested in normal or sharing much of anything. "Thanks for answering my call."

"I always try to answer yours."

Mack knew that response was about the kindest thing Griff would ever say to anybody. He turned onto the side road leading toward the freeway, increasing his speed. "Hey, I met someone who said she knew you from college." Griff didn't respond so he continued. "Scarlett Lily."

He heard an audible intake from Griff. Mack paused, thinking this was the strongest response he'd ever gotten from his brother and wondering if his brother would reveal anything to him.

"And?" was all he got.

"She asked me to tell you ..." How had she phrased it? Thoughts of Sariah pushed other conversations to the back of his mind. "That she asked about you."

"Hmm." Griff sort of grunted.

"What's the story there, bro?"

"Nothing. Scarlett's ... nice."

"Nice? I think a lot of men would have a better description for Scarlett Lily than 'nice'." Mack was goading him now and it wasn't nice, but Scarlett obviously felt something for his brother and he would love to see his brother fall in love. Then again, it probably wasn't fair to Scarlett to push a hardened man like Griff on her. She did seem like a very nice person.

"Did you need something?"

Classic Griff. But Mack did need something. "Yeah, I, um, need some info, a home address, work address, phone number, whatever you can give me."

"Why and on who?"

"Sariah Udy." The who was so much easier to explain than the why. There was absolutely no way to explain to Griff how Sariah looked at him, how he'd fallen for her, why he couldn't get her out of his mind. Not that Mack cared that Griff would think he was a wimp, which Griff would. It was simply that falling for a woman wasn't in Griff's makeup. He had no point of reference for it. It was much better for Scarlett Lily that she not see Griff again.

Mack cruised onto the freeway, pushing the buttons so his vehicle would basically drive itself.

Griff was still waiting. "Why?" he asked again.

"I love her," Mack sputtered out. Oh, no! He didn't love her, love her. He didn't even know her. But he had to get to know her.

"What?" Griff grunted, his voice filled with disgust. "You're too young to know what love is."

"Please help me find her, Griff." He ignored the reference to his youth. He was the baby of the family, but he was twenty-five, self-sufficient, and he knew his own mind.

"Does she want to be found?"

"I think so. It's her brother-in-law who's blocking me."

"Hyde Metcalf?"

"You know who she is?"

"I watch the news occasionally," Griff said drily.

"Do you watch Scarlett Lily occasionally?" Mack knew he shouldn't have said that the instant the words were out.

"Do you want help or not?" Griff's voice had gotten chillier and more raw than normal.

"Please, Griff. I just need to talk to Sariah. You know me, I'll leave her alone if she's not interested."

Griff waited, let him sweat it out. He only needed to lightly touch the steering wheel to keep his car speeding along with traffic, but his grip on the steering wheel got tighter and tighter.

"Please," he said again.

"I'll see what I can find." Griff hung up without a goodbye.

The conversation wasn't bad as far as conversations with Griff went and Mack felt a giddy happiness inside. Griff was the best at finding info. Soon Mack would be knocking on Sariah Udy's door.

Sariah made sure Teresa was settled in one of the spare bedrooms at Hyde's condo, her stomach churning the entire time. She couldn't get the memory of Scarlett Lily kissing Mack's jaw out of her mind. His jaw. That perfect jaw Sariah would love to touch with her fingertips. And Scarlett Lily had touched it with her lips.

Why had Sariah deluded herself into thinking Mack Quinn was special or that she was special to him? She hated how inexperienced and vulnerable she was. A few looks and kind words and Mack had captured her heart. She had to learn how to be stronger, somehow.

"Good night, sweetheart," Teresa said. "Don't you worry about me. I'm just tired."

"Okay. See you in the morning."

Teresa peered at her from the bed. "Are you going to tell me more about that big, handsome guy?"

Sariah shook her head. "Like I said, there's nothing to tell."

"I think there is."

She blew out a breath and admitted quietly, "I saw him with Scarlett Lily as we were leaving. She kissed his jaw."

"Did it look intimate or like a famous Hollywood person being all cheesy and kissing everybody? I've known a lot of those types in my life."

"It looked intimate." Sariah hated to admit the truth, but the exchange had looked very intimate and neither Mack nor Scarlett Lily had a reputation for being a flirt or a player. The way

Mack had watched Scarlett walk away bothered her as much as them being so close and Scarlett kissing him.

"Sorry, love."

"Thanks." Sariah slipped out the door, shutting it quietly behind her. She loved Teresa like a favorite aunt. Sometimes taking care of her was exhausting, but mostly it was fun to be with her, and the woman genuinely loved her. She was glad she'd talked to somebody about her Mack dreams being crushed.

Padding into the spacious living area, she looked out at the view of Atlanta, the lights sparkling below Hyde's high-rise condo.

Hyde and Lily were on the couch, snuggled up. Sariah pivoted. She'd go back and hang out with Teresa some more rather than interrupt their alone time. She knew they didn't get to be together often enough.

"Sariah?" Hyde's voice stopped her.

She whirled back. "Hey. Don't let me interrupt the smooch fest."

Lily laughed. "We were just talking. Get in here and talk to us."

Only sisters could boss somebody around like that. At least talking with them would get her mind off of Mack. She settled into the overstuffed chair across from them and smiled. "So, tell me about the wedding plans."

Lily shook her head. "Not right now. Tell us about Mack Quinn."

Sariah's stomach leapt and then plunged immediately. Obviously, she wasn't going to get her mind off of him. A couple hours ago she would've been ecstatic to talk about Mack, but not now.

Hyde's brows were drawn together. He didn't look mad, more concerned.

"Mack Quinn?" she asked, feigning innocence. Would Teresa have ratted her out about the garden interlude? She couldn't think of when Teresa would've been alone with Hyde or Lily, except for that brief time that Sariah had gone back to try to find Mack ... and seen him with Scarlett Lily. Schnikies, she hated that brief time.

"We've seen the way he looks at you," Lily said.

"He's asked me a couple of times about you," Hyde admitted.

"What?" Sariah could barely keep her seat.

Hyde stared at her as only an older brother could stare at her. "After a couple of games. Has he been checking you out all season?"

"I guess." It didn't matter now, but why hadn't Hyde told her? "He asked you about me? Why didn't you tell me?"

Hyde shifted and glanced at Lily. "I didn't want him to hurt you."

Sariah blinked at him. Mack was huge and muscular, but he would never hurt her physically. The only way he could hurt her ... he'd done at the party tonight. Two-timing her just like Tyler had done. She knew exactly why Hyde was worried and any frustration at him not telling her about Mack asking about her died quickly. Especially when Mack was obviously not the man she thought he was.

"Thanks for watching out for me, Hyde," she whispered.

Hyde kept giving her these penetrating stares, only bested by

Lily's more penetrating stares. "If you … like him, I can give him your number. I know you're an adult and I don't want to treat you like you're not. I just know he and the Quinn family are high profile and after what you went through, I didn't want to expose you to that."

Did she *like* Mack? She liked everything about him, except for Scarlett Lily kissing him in such a public setting. "No. You're right. It's for the best. I wouldn't want to be put on display again." She tugged at the hair covering her disfigured right ear and side of her neck. "You ready to head to the hotel, sis?" She needed to get out of here. Sleep off this pain. Her silly fascination with Mack was over. She knew it couldn't go anywhere, so why did it hurt so bad?

Hyde stood, pulling Lily to her feet. "I should've dropped you both off at the hotel earlier. I just wanted a little more time with my beautiful fiancée."

"Wouldn't want to deny you that." Lily winked at him. "Teresa was worn out. We'll get an Uber, no worries."

Hyde pulled out his phone and brought up the app. Sariah said goodbye to Hyde and hurried to the front entry. Thankfully the condo was big enough they could have some privacy to say their goodnights. Unfortunately, it wasn't big enough for her to miss hearing the sound of their kissing, soft laughs, and smitten voices. Oh, to find a love like Hyde and Lily's. Obviously, it wasn't in the cards for her. Sariah pushed a hand against her heart, but it still felt tight and painful.

CHAPTER SEVEN

Two weeks had passed since Mack had seen Sariah. Griff had finally, finally got him some information. He didn't blame Griff, not at all, he'd just been impatient because he wanted to see Sariah. His brother had been busy taking down a trafficking ring in Belize and rescuing dozens of women and children. His brother was a hero many times over, and Mack was proud of him. He still wondered what had happened with him and Scarlett Lily, but knew he'd get nothing out of Griff. Bringing up Scarlett's reference to tickling Griff might get Mack a reaction, but guaranteed it would tick Griff off. Most people tried very hard never to tick Griff off.

Mack was in a rented Cherokee, driving west from Denver up I-70 into the mountains toward the little town of Georgetown. Sariah's hometown. He couldn't stop thanking Griff, and Heavenly Father, in his head. He had Sariah's address. The only worry was if she was actually here. Hyde had said she lived in Denver.

Was she working in Denver, going to school in Denver? Most people at twenty-one or twenty-two wouldn't still be living at home. But this was his only hope of finding her. Griff had only given him this address, and told him gruffly to stop saying thank you.

The river flowed next to the freeway, speeding along with spring runoff. Mack rarely saw traffic this sparse in Atlanta, especially on a Friday at noon. It was a pretty spring day. The leaves were just budding on the trees at this higher elevation, but there were so many pine trees in these mountains it still looked lush and green. He'd been to Denver quite a few times but he'd never seen this part of the area and he loved it. Not quite as green as Georgia, but these towering mountains were unreal.

He took the turn for Georgetown and drove past a mountain lake and through a very quiet town. The mountains sheltered the town, towering above it on all sides. It fit Sariah perfectly—beautiful, peaceful, guarded, and unassuming.

He followed Siri's directions, stopping at a small house on the edge of the town's park. The grass was still brown from winter and a few piles of snow remained. How cool was that? Mack had grown up in Rhode Island and loved the snow. He'd missed it since going to college in Texas and living in Georgia the past couple of years.

Slowly climbing from the vehicle, he felt the stirring of nerves and the crisp air wrapping around him. What would Sariah think of him chasing her down like this? What would her family think? Would they call Hyde, find out he'd already been warned away, and tell him to leave? Mack hated confrontation and never sought out a fight, but Sariah was worth fighting for.

He strode to the front door. There was a small cement spot that served as the outside entry, but it was flat without any front porch. He was surprised Hyde or Lily hadn't fixed up the drooping family home with all the money they surely had, but maybe Lily and Sariah's parents were too prideful to accept help like that. Not seeing a doorbell, he rapped his knuckles on the door and it immediately sprung open. A small boy stared up at him, his dark eyes wide with hero worship. "You're Mack Quinn."

Mack nodded. "Hi." He stuck his hand out. "Nice to meet you."

The little guy put his small hand in Mack's palm and shook it vigorously. He pulled back and leapt into the air, did a little dance, and yelled, "Mack Quinn came to see me! Yes!"

Mack chuckled. He hoped it wouldn't break the kid's heart when he found out Mack was here for his sister.

"Wait right here," the kid demanded, holding up both palms. "I've got to find your card and have you sign it." He danced back into the house singing, "Mack Quinn is *he-ere!*"

Mack stood in the open doorway, not sure what to do but wait. A tall older, teenage boy appeared, with two smaller teenage girls with him. The entire family was olive-skinned with dark hair and eyes like Sariah and Lily. Possibly Italian heritage. They all gawked at him for a second.

Mack put out his hand. "Mack Quinn. I'm here to see Sariah."

The boy's eyes widened in understanding. "Caleb Udy." He shook his hand and tilted his head to his sisters. "Trudy and Mary."

"Hi." Mack shook their hands quickly.

"Sorry about Josh. He's obsessed with football."

"He's a cute kid." Mack loved that Sariah had a large family like him. He'd come from much more affluent circumstances but at least they had family size in common. It could be a point in his favor.

"How do you know Sariah?" Caleb asked.

"I saw you talking to her after one of Hyde's games," Mary piped in, her tone more accusatory then welcoming.

"I've ... seen her at a lot of games, but I officially met her at a party a couple weeks ago," Mack tried to explain. "Are your parents here?"

They all shook their heads. "Dad's at work and Mom's grocery shopping with our brother, Brandon. It's early out on Friday so I'm babysitting," Caleb explained.

"You don't need to babysit us." Trudy rolled her eyes and pushed out one hip. She looked the most like Sariah.

"Why don't you just call or text Sariah if you 'know her'?" Mary made quote fingers with her hands and her dark eyes were full of sass.

"I'd love to. Will you give me her number?"

Mary gave him a challenging glare. "Do you know how many guys want her number? I'm not stupid."

Mack hid a grimace. Her little sister obviously saw right through him. The whole family seemed to have a lot of fire in them.

Josh rushed back into the room and plowed through his siblings, triumphantly holding up Mack's football trading card. "Can you sign it, please, Mr. Quinn, please?"

The siblings all regarded their little brother with fond looks; it reminded Mack of how his siblings were always so good to him. There was also a protective feeling these Udy siblings had and Mack remembered hearing about the traumatic accident that happened to Josh and Caleb last year. No wonder the siblings wanted to protect him. For Mack, it had been the speech impediment and complete silence for years. It had made his brothers crazy protective of him, getting in lots of fights. Luckily, Navy, the oldest, was in middle school and never saw or heard about the bullying. She would've torn somebody apart.

"Of course." Mack took the card and the pen Josh thrust at him. He signed his name and handed it back. "I should've brought you some hats and sweatshirts." What had he been thinking? Gifts for the family would've come in handy right about now. They obviously didn't have much financially, and Josh seemed to be the only one who wasn't suspicious of him.

Caleb waved a hand at that. "Hyde gives us lots of stuff."

Hyde. Oh, yeah. The Hyde that had warned Mack to stay away from Sariah. Hyde wasn't going to like this at all, but Mack couldn't dwell on that. He was an adult. Sariah was an adult. He was going to find Sariah and talk to her no matter what obstacles were put in his path.

"Can you please give me her number?" He directed the question to Caleb, obviously the oldest at home and the one in charge.

"If some dude, bigger than your house, showed up asking for your sister's number, would you give it to him?" Caleb asked.

Mack hated to admit that he wouldn't.

"This isn't just some big dude, this is Mack Quinn," Josh protested. "Best offensive lineman in the world! He protects the Rocket and makes it possible for Hyde to get perfect passes. You give him whatever he wants." Josh jutted his chin out and looked so cute Mack had to refrain from picking him up and giving him a quick hug.

The girls both smiled patiently. Caleb squatted down next to his little brother. "Josh ... you know I'd do anything for you, but I'm trying to protect Sariah here."

"Why would Sariah need protection from Mack Quinn?"

"Just because somebody's a great football player doesn't mean they're a good person."

Mack's eyebrows rose. He wanted to start calling character witnesses. He tried very hard to be a good person and these loyal siblings of Sariah's were going to block him from finding her just like Hyde had. Maybe he was the one in the wrong here, but he yearned for Sariah like he'd never yearned for a person. He wanted to ask his brother Kaleb to write a song about it. Then he could sing it for Sariah and maybe win her over. He was no Kaleb Quinn, but he had a decent voice.

"You're a good guy, aren't you, Mr. Quinn?" Josh demanded.

"I like to think so."

"You're not going to hurt Sariah, are you?"

Mack swallowed hard. "I promise you, Josh, that I would never do anything to hurt Sariah. I care for her deeply."

The sisters were looking a little less defensive but still wary. Caleb stood and shrugged his shoulders. "Look man, I'm not trying to be a jerk, it's just Sariah ... she's pretty special to us and she's been through a lot."

"Hyde said something similar," Mack admitted.

Caleb's eyes narrowed. "So, you already asked Hyde for her number and he told you no?"

Dang, this kid was quick. Mack nodded, not able to lie.

"I'm sorry." Caleb picked Josh up and ushered him back from the door. The girls stepped back and Caleb moved to swing the door closed.

"Please," Mack begged.

"She lives with Hyde's mama, Teresa," Josh yelled.

"Josh," all the other siblings reprimanded.

"Thank you," Mack said.

Caleb firmly shut the door on him. That hadn't gone too well, but at least he had another lead. He called Griff and luckily his brother answered.

"What now?" Griff asked.

"I need an address for Teresa Metcalf's home. I think it's near Denver."

Griff exhaled loudly. "I'll text it to you, but no more."

"Thanks, bro."

Griff hung up.

Mack hoped he wasn't making his brother break laws but this information was something he seriously needed to know. *No more*, echoed in his head. If he didn't find Sariah at Teresa's house, what would he do? Start wandering the streets of Denver asking if anyone knew her?

His phone beeped and he had to wait until he exited the canyon and could pull off the freeway in the first little town. The address was in Golden, Colorado. He hoped that wasn't too far away. When he plugged it in and saw he was already in Golden, he thought maybe things were finally going his way. Bless that little Josh for idolizing him and giving him what he needed and Griff for probably bending rules he shouldn't bend to find him the information.

He followed Siri's voice along quiet city streets, back up a hill closer to the mountainside. The cul-de-sac was affluent, but Hyde's mom's house was definitely the nicest and the biggest. He loved the flow of the redbrick two-story and all the windows. The landscaping was amazing with spring flowers straining to peek out. He jumped from his rental and hurried to the door. Teresa had smiled at him at the party at Bucky's. Even if Sariah wasn't here, maybe Teresa wouldn't turn him away.

He pushed the doorbell and waited impatiently. A few seconds later the door swung open. Two ladies stood staring at him. He recognized the blonde as Teresa but didn't know the shorter, darker-haired lady.

"I know you," Teresa said.

"Lucky you." The other lady pumped her eyebrows and looked him over.

"Mack Quinn." Mack stuck out his hand. Both the ladies took turns shaking his hand.

"Teresa," Hyde's mom murmured.

"Auntie Allie," the dark-haired lady said.

"We didn't officially meet but I was with Sariah last week at Bucky's party ... in the gardens."

"Lucky Sariah," Allie said.

Teresa's blue eyes lit with understanding but then they narrowed quickly. "Sariah saw you kissing Scarlett Lily." She folded her arms across her chest and tilted her head in an obvious challenge. "What do you have to say for yourself, young man?"

"Whoa." Mack held up his hands. "No. I promise I did not kiss Scarlett Lily." Had Sariah seen him talking with Scarlett? Oh, no. What if it hurt her?

They both glared imperiously at him, Allie mimicking her friend's defensive stance.

"She kissed my jaw," he explained. "She dated my brother, Griff, and wanted me to give him a message."

Their stance softened perceptively.

"I promise I am not dating Scarlett. I couldn't think of dating someone else when my head is so full of Sariah."

Allie placed a hand on her heart. "Oh, that was sweet."

"Is she here?" he asked quickly, maybe too quickly as the women exchanged a wary look.

"No, she's not," Teresa said. "She's at ... school."

"Oh." Of course, she wouldn't be home in the middle of the day. "Could you give me her number, or if you don't feel comfortable with that, I could leave my number." These two were the most receptive of anyone, besides Josh. "I need to talk to her."

They exchanged a look then finally Teresa said, "You can give us your number."

"Thank you." Mack hoped he didn't look like an eager puppy dog. He hurriedly wrote his number on the notepad they gave him, along with a, *Please, call me, Mack Quinn*, and handed it back. "Please tell her I'm not with Scarlett."

"Did you travel from Georgia just to find our girl?" Allie demanded.

Mack hesitated, not sure how desperate he wanted to look, but he was desperate, for Sariah. Finally, he nodded.

Allie pursed her lips. "I kind of like him."

Mack smiled.

"We'll give her your number, and tell her you'll go to any lengths to talk to her," Allie said.

"Thanks." Mack backed away from the door. He was tempted to camp in the driveway. It was only 12:30. He wondered how long her school went.

"Bye."

Teresa started to close the door but Allie stopped her and said, "If I were you, I'd go get a massage to pass the time."

"A massage?"

Allie nodded and winked. "Massage Therapy Institute of Denver."

Mack's pulse jumped. Sariah was in school to be a massage therapist. That fit what he thought he knew of her and this was a fabulous lead. "Thank you," he called to Allie.

"See you soon." The door closed, but he could hear the two women giggling together. They hadn't given him Sariah's number, but this was almost as good. They had his number and he knew where she was going to school. He'd call and get a massage appointment. Sariah would have to talk to him then. A massage from Sariah? His pulse jumped and his entire body warmed as he imagined lying on a massage bed with Sariah's hands working on his bare back. His mama would be appalled at the visions he started having of him sitting up on the bed and pulling her close, without a shirt on. He shook his head to clear it and focused on finding Sariah.

CHAPTER EIGHT

Mack asked Siri to navigate him to the Massage Therapy Institute. She informed him they were twenty-five minutes away. He hit go and asked her to call the Massage Therapy Institute as he drove east toward Denver. A woman's voice answered with a crisp, "Massage Therapy Institute of Denver. How may I help you?"

"I'd like to schedule a massage with Sariah Udy."

"I can schedule a massage for you with one of our students but we don't schedule for a particular person. I apologize. Would you still like an appointment?"

Mack gritted his teeth. Apparently, this breakthrough was going to be similar to the others and not an easy route to Sariah. "How late can I schedule a massage appointment?"

"Our last appointments begin at five p.m., sir."

"If I schedule a massage, is there a chance Sariah will be my therapist?"

"A slim chance, sir, we have dozens of students at the level of performing massages for the public."

"But Sariah is one of them."

She hesitated then admitted, "Yes, sir, she is."

At least he had a chance of his therapist being Sariah. What did he have to lose? He'd get a massage, pass the time until Sariah was done with school. "Please schedule me for a massage."

"What time, sir?"

He glanced at the clock. It was now after one and he was at least thirty minutes from the school. "Do you have an opening at two?"

"Yes."

"That will work."

"Your name, sir?"

"Mack Quinn."

"We'll see you at two p.m."

"Thank you." Mack disconnected. He drove through a Kneaders and ordered several sandwiches and a fruit smoothie. Stuffing the food down as he finished following Siri's directions to the massage institute, he made sure to chew a bunch of breath mints on the off-chance he found Sariah.

He parked next to the massage school and a few minutes before two walked through the glass doors and up to the reception area. It was nothing fancy but it was clean and looked professional. Sariah was becoming a massage therapist. How great was that?

"Hi." He smiled at the older lady manning the desk. "I called for an appointment at two? Mack Quinn."

The lady nodded to him, not smiling. She was dressed in a navy-blue business suit and her hair was in a severe bun. "Yes, please follow me, sir." Her voice was as crisp as on the phone and her movements were fast and jerky.

Mack hurried to keep up with her as she led him through the reception area, down a short hallway, and edged open a door to a small therapy room. The tranquil sound of a waterfall and the scent of lavender oozed from the dimly lit room.

"Please undress completely, cover your lower half with the sheet, and lay face down."

Mack's eyes widened. "Um ... I only want an upper body massage." He had had hundreds of full body massages throughout his football career, they were a necessity for recovery, but the thought of being naked with Sariah in the same room didn't sit right with him at all.

Her eyes narrowed. "Fine, undress from the waist up. The attendant will knock before entering." She whirled and tapped away from him.

Wow, apparently you didn't need people skills to be a receptionist at a massage therapy school. Mack closed the door, peeled off his shirt, and laid face down on the bed. His body covered the entire bed and his feet hung off the end. He figured he didn't need the sheet with his pants still on.

Moments later, there was a soft tap on the door. "May I come in?" It was a male voice. Ah, no.

"Yeah," Mack grunted.

The man entered, introduced himself, asked where Mack was feeling tight, etc. Mack responded and tried to relax as the man gave him a deep tissue massage. The guy was good, but Mack just wanted to find Sariah. He finally worked up the nerve to ask, "Do you know Sariah Udy?"

"Yes, sir, I do."

"Is there any way I could speak to her?"

"I'm sorry. Sariah's with a client right now."

The man continued his kneading of Mack's back, shoulders, and neck. When he finished, he told Mack to take his time getting up and to drink the water bottle he'd left for him then thanked him for coming.

Mack thought he responded appropriately, but his mind was searching for Sariah. He sat up quick, saw stars for a second, and chugged the water bottle. Hurrying to put his shirt on, he rushed out the door and down the hallway. Just his luck the same, stern lady was at the reception desk.

"How was your massage, sir?"

"It was great." Mack pulled out his wallet and paid the crazy low rate of thirty dollars for a full-hour massage and left a thirty-dollar tip. "Can I please schedule another one?"

"Of course." She tapped on her computer. "What date and time please?"

"Right now," Mack said.

Her sharp gaze darted to him.

"Three o'clock, please."

"You're still hoping to find Sariah Udy?"

"Yes, ma'am."

She shook her head and rolled her eyes. Then she tapped on her screen some more and tilted her head. "This way, please."

He followed her down the short hallway to a different room. The smells and the waterfall imitation sounds were the same, must be a standard for the school. He shut the door, took off his shirt, and laid down again, praying, *Please be Sariah, please be Sariah.*

The soft tap came on the door. "May I come in?" A female voice this time, but not the one he hoped for.

"Sure," Mack grunted.

The woman came in and started asking him questions and working on him. Mack got through the questions before he started asking his own. "Do you know Sariah Udy?"

"Yes," her voice became more cautious and Mack wondered if everyone in the universe was protective of his girl. Okay, not his girl, but maybe someday his girl.

"Could you get a message to her for me?"

"Maybe. What's the message?"

"Tell her Mack Quinn is here and I'm going to keep getting massages until she is my therapist or school is over. If I don't find her before school is over today can she please meet me out front at six?"

The girl worked a spot in his upper back with her elbow for a few seconds before replying, "I'll give her the message. You play for the Patriots, right?"

"Yeah."

The rest of the massage was spent talking football. Mack liked the massage and the talk, but he was too keyed up about finding Sariah to truly relax or focus on anything else.

The lady finished, thanked him, gave him the spiel about standing up slowly along with a water bottle. Mack stood, downed the water, grabbed his shirt, and hurried back to the reception desk.

Tight-bun reception lady took his credit card, he signed and added a tip then he asked her for a four o'clock appointment.

"Do you know how to give up?" she asked him tightly, letting her professional demeanor slip a little bit.

"No, ma'am."

The lady's lips curved in what might have been a smile, but Mack didn't want to assume too much. Then she pushed out a sigh, tapped the computer some more and did her crisp, "Follow me," and staccato down the hallway.

Third room, same smells, sound, and bed. Mack was getting

tired from flying in this morning, all the runaround today, the massages, and the soothing smells and sounds. If this wasn't Sariah, he wouldn't talk, he'd take a nap instead. He peeled off his shirt, the scents of different oils they'd worked into his back probably overpowered his Taylor cologne that Navy had picked out for him. In his sister's words, "You need this smell, little bro, manly and succulent."

Laying down on the bed, he shut his eyes and prayed for Sariah to come in. If it wasn't her, he might give up on the last hour and just rest in his rented Cherokee until six when she should be done with school, but what if he missed her?

The tap came at the door and a female voice, "May I come in?"

The disappointment that it wasn't Sariah rushed over him. Maybe the stern bun lady was right and he needed to stop being so persistent. A worse thought nagged at him, maybe the woman he thought was his destiny really wasn't.

Sariah loved her schooling and her classmates and teachers. They learned and practiced on each other in the mornings, then throughout the afternoon they practiced on real people, if people came in. If not, they practiced on each other some more. It was better to work on real people because they knew each other too well, and sometimes they even got tips, which was really nice.

Friday afternoon she had a break with no client from four to five. Everybody else was busy so her instructor told her to take a break and read up on techniques. She headed back to the main classroom, drank some water, and checked her phone quick.

Her eyebrows rose when she saw she had seventeen texts and many missed calls. Fear rushed through her. Had something happened? Rather than check the texts, she pressed call back on the phone call from Caleb.

"What's up?" she asked him, clinging to the phone. They'd had a horrid scare last spring when Josh and Caleb had been in a car accident where Josh ended up in a coma.

"Mack Quinn came here," Caleb said.

"What?" She gripped the phone even more tightly. Nothing was wrong with her family, but this news still made her stomach tumble. Mack Quinn went to her house and she missed him?

"Yeah. He stopped by and Josh gushed all over him. Why would he come here, sis?"

"I don't know. He and I have ... talked a couple of times." Mack had come for her! Did that mean he didn't like Scarlett Lily? She'd watched social media and Google diligently but had seen nothing indicating they were dating. Scarlett was in California finishing up a movie, so maybe they just hadn't had the time to be together.

"Hmm. He wanted your number but when I asked why he hadn't gotten it from Hyde he admitted he'd tried. If Hyde shut him down, I didn't want to give him anything, you know?" He paused. "Did you want me to give it to him, sis?"

"I ... I'm as confused as a baseball player at a lacrosse game." She pushed her hair back from the right side and touched the mottled skin on her neck. Mack Quinn. She'd love to see him again, talk to him, but the thought of going somewhere with him and having someone take pictures of her, maybe see her deformity and shout how she wasn't worthy of perfection like Mack Quinn's ... she couldn't take that again.

"Josh told him you lived with Teresa. I wanted you to have a head's up."

"Thanks," she murmured, her thoughts bouncing all over the place, but they were all centered on Mack.

"He seems like a nice guy," Caleb said.

"Yeah, he does."

"Talk to you later. Be careful, sis."

"I will. Love you."

"You too." Caleb disconnected.

Sariah looked through her texts and saw a bunch from Caleb, Trudy, and Mary and a few from Aunt Allie. Teresa didn't text but she'd called. Sariah hit the call back on her number.

"Sariah, girl!" Teresa screamed excitedly into the phone.

"I never have to doubt how much you like me," Sariah said.

"Of course, I adore you." Teresa laughed. "Mack Quinn came here for you."

"H-he did?" Persistent, wasn't he?

"He's pretty hot, my girl, and he said he isn't with Scarlett Lily. Do you like him?"

"What do you mean he isn't with Scarlett Lily?" She ignored the question.

"That's what he said when I questioned him about kissing her at the party. Said she wants his brother, Griff."

"Oh." Sariah's brain felt like it was exploding. She sank into a chair, grateful no one else was in the room. "What else did he say?"

"He wanted your number but we didn't know about that so he gave us his number. Oh, and Allie told him to go get a massage. Did he show up at your school?"

Sariah's gaze darted around the classroom, as if he would appear suddenly. She wished he would. It seemed he was focused on finding her. Her heart fluttered at the thought.

Jane rushed into the room. "Sariah! You'll never guess who I just did a massage on."

"I've got to scatter, Teresa."

"Okay, love. Let us know what happens."

"I will, thanks." She hung up the phone, stood on quivering legs, and faced Jane. "Mack Quinn?" she asked.

"Yes! How'd you know? He asked about you."

"He did?"

Jane nodded, her blue eyes wide. "Oh, my goodness Sariah, he's so tough. I've never worked on a body like that. Muscles upon muscles."

Sariah was having a hard time breathing, imagining Mack with no shirt on. What would those muscles look and feel like?

"Joseph told me he worked on him the hour before me and he asked for you then. And get this, I just saw him walk into another room. Georgina's with him, but I just know he's trying to find you, getting massage after massage until he does. Do you want to go relieve her of her duties?" Jane giggled and squeezed her hand.

Sariah was having an out of body experience. Mack had traveled to Colorado and was obviously pursuing any lead to find her. She was hot and cold all over. Did she want to give him a massage? Yes!

"Sariah?" Jane's eyes lost their sparkle. "Don't you want to see him? It might take the entire school to protect you from him, but you know we would."

Sariah shook her head and then nodded. "No, I mean, yes, please, I definitely want to dance my fingers over muscles upon muscles."

Jane grinned again, taking her hand and tugging her toward the hallway that led to the treatment rooms. Sariah increased her pace. She should go freshen her makeup, spritz on body splash, make sure she didn't have spinach from her lunch salad in her teeth, but the pull of Mack was too much.

They reached treatment room seven and Jane tapped softly on the door.

"Yes?" Georgina asked.

Jane opened the door. "I need you," Jane lied.

Sariah stared at Mack lying face down on the massage table. His body took up the bed and then some. He had on some fitted dark gray chinos, and she was grateful he wasn't completely undressed like most clients would be. She didn't know if she could've handled seeing more of him than she already could. Jane had understated how many muscles he had and how fabulous those muscles looked. She froze in the doorway, aware Jane and Georgina were having a quiet conversation, but not registering any of it. She wanted to touch Mack Quinn, but more than that she wanted him to sit up and look at her, talk to her, hold her. Okay, her wants were piling up too quick.

"You'll share the tip with Georgina?" Jane whispered to her.

"You can have all the tip," Sariah said.

At the sound of her voice, Mack pushed up and in one swift move was on his feet. "Sariah?"

Jane shoved her into the room and shut the door. Sariah would've fallen, but it was a small room and Mack reached out and steadied her with a hand on her elbow. His handsome face split in a grin. "Sariah. I've been looking for you."

She stepped back and leaned against the counter that held their supplies. She wanted to hug him, savor each one of those beautifully-sculpted muscles, but she needed to keep her head on right now. "So I've heard."

His smile grew, but his blue eyes looked uncertain, as if he worried she'd turn him away.

"Do you want to continue with your massage, Mr. Quinn?" she asked.

He shook his head. "No, I want to talk to you."

"Ah, so you aren't interested in my expert massage techniques?"

"Oh, I'm interested, and I'll talk you into a massage sometime soon, but right now all I want to do is look at your beautiful face and beg you to go to dinner tonight."

Her heart was thumping quickly, but nerves also assaulted her. She pulled her hair tight to the right side of her neck, making sure her ear was covered. He wouldn't think she was beautiful if he saw her scars, but he'd come all this way and he was so charming and appealing to her. He dwarfed her physically but she felt no fear around him, besides the fear of him seeing her burns. She felt a pull to stay close to him, let him protect her and smile at her like he was doing right now.

"Hmm, dinner," she forced some sass into her tone. "I might be persuaded. Give me your top picks."

He chuckled. "I couldn't care less. I'd eat McDonald's if it meant spending time with you."

She wrinkled her nose, though her heart soared. He wanted to spend time with her. "Not a huge fan of McDonald's but ... okay."

He laughed louder. "No, I meant, McDonald's isn't my top pick, but I'd eat anywhere to be with you."

"Do you like Thai food?"

"Sure." He lifted and lowered his broad shoulders.

Sariah's mouth went dry as she glanced over his muscular upper body. She wished he'd let her massage him, but him saying that he wanted to look at her and talk to her meant a lot. "I know a good Thai place that's close by."

Mack took a step closer and she could hardly catch a breath. What she wouldn't give to put her hand on one of his bulging pectoralis muscles then slide her fingers up to his broad shoulders.

"Close by, across the ocean," his voice was low and melodious. "I don't care. I just want to be with you."

"You are a lot more forward than I thought you were."

"What do you mean?" He bent down closer to her.

"You spent months catching my gaze before and after games, not even mustering up the courage to talk to me. Then you throw propriety to the wind and travel across the country to find me. Why?"

He nodded. "I thought maybe I was just being silly, thinking there was this connection between us as I stared at you, but after talking to you at that party ... I haven't been able to get you out of my mind. I had to find you and see if you're who I think you are."

She let herself rest her hand on his forearm. It was so big, tough, and manly she had to fight not to massage it under her fingertips. "And who do you think I am?"

He smiled softly. "My dream girl."

Sariah had to swallow hard. "I guess we'll see."

"Yes, *we* will." His smile grew. "Any chance severe bun-lady will let you leave early?"

"Severe bun ..." Sariah laughed. "Miriam? Probably not."

He reclined back against the side of the bed, wrapped both hands around her hips, and pulled her toward him. Sariah's breath caught and her arms and legs trembled. Who knew being close to a giant of a man could be this exhilarating?

"Any chance you'll give me a quick hug for making such an effort to find you?" Mack said so quietly she could barely hear him.

Sariah wanted to hug him until the appointment time ran out, but she had held herself in check around men for too long. She couldn't simply change her M.O. and throw her arms around this perfect man, who was obviously chasing her.

She straightened away from him and retreated back to the counter, leaning against it to support herself. Mack's face flashed disappointment but he didn't move toward her. Thank heavens or she'd probably have yielded. Every part of her wanted to lay her cheek against that shredded chest and hang on.

"A flight across the country doesn't give you those kinds of privileges," she tried to be sassy but her heart was beating so fast the words came out all breathy and full of longing.

Mack nodded. "Is there any hope of me earning a hug?"

She arched her eyebrows. "Is a hug all you're after, big boy?"

His lips curved into the most irresistible smirk. He stood up straight and the sheer glory of his build overwhelmed and thrilled her. "No." He took a step closer. Sariah tilted her head back to maintain eye contact. "Any man who chases a woman across the country would be a fool to not beg for a kiss at some point."

Sariah's stomach swooped and then filled with heat. She hoped her face didn't reveal that if he kept being so enticing, she'd kiss him before they went on a single date.

"Hmm," she said. "I guess we'll see how good your begging skills are."

"They're pretty good. I was the youngest after all."

Sariah laughed thinking of Josh and how he almost always got his way. "You've got to watch out for those babies of the family." Though there was nothing childlike about him.

"We're pretty irresistible." He leaned closer and Sariah lost all rational thought and the ability to breathe.

Mack reached up and tenderly touched her right cheek. "You're so beautiful," he murmured. His hand trailed back, pushing at the hair covering the right side of her face.

"Stop!" Sariah screamed, ducking out of his reach.

The door burst open and Joseph stood there. "Sariah? Did he hurt you?"

Mack was eight inches taller and at least a hundred pounds heavier than Joseph. It was nice but really stupid of Joseph to stand up for her.

"No," she whispered. She glanced back at Mack. His face was full of confusion and regret.

"I'm sorry, Sariah. I didn't mean to ..." Mack's voice trailed off as it was obvious he had no clue what he'd done.

Sariah felt horrible for the way she'd reacted ... but the thought of Mack seeing or touching her scars. Her stomach soured and she backed further away from him. Joseph put a reassuring arm around her.

Miriam appeared in the hallway. "What's going on here?" she demanded.

"Nothing," Sariah insisted. How could she explain why she'd screamed? She didn't want anyone thinking Mack would hurt her. She wanted to erase the worried look from his eyes, rewind time to a few minutes ago when it was just them bantering, and somehow react differently yet still protect her secret.

"It's time you go, Mr. Quinn." Miriam folded her arms across her chest.

Mack stared at Sariah, ignoring everyone else.

"I'm sorry," she murmured. "I ... overreacted."

He nodded tightly, obviously still confused how she could react that extremely to him brushing her hair from her face. She never wanted him to see her scars. It was irrational and extreme but she wanted him to keep thinking she was beautiful.

She straightened her shoulders and tried to think how to salvage the situation. The best thing to do would be to get Mack out of here and talk to him later, but what would she say? "I'll see you out front at six."

"Sariah." Joseph pulled her around to face him. "You don't want to go out with a man who would hurt you."

Sariah shook her head. "Mack would never hurt me. I ... I can't explain. This is on me." She glanced back at Mack. He stood there looking so strong and appealing, but not threatening. She knew he wouldn't hurt her, but what made her think she could date someone like him and not have her deformity be an issue? She'd never fit in that perfect wives and girlfriends club of football players. She almost told him she couldn't go to dinner, but that wasn't fair to him.

Instead, she gave him a forced smile and pushed past Joseph and Miriam, hurrying to the women's bathroom. She barely made it into a stall before hot tears pricked at her eyes. She couldn't date Mack, and every part of her wanted to.

CHAPTER NINE

Mack watched Sariah leave, certain this wasn't his moment to chase after her, though that was the only thing he wanted to do. He'd finally found her and she'd been as witty and beautiful as he'd imagined. He knew she was responding well to him, then as he went to brush her hair from her face, she'd come apart. There must be some reason she kept her thick hair over the right side of her face and neck. He couldn't think of a time he hadn't seen it down and swooping to the right. He'd be very careful not to try moving it again, but he wished she'd confide in him. What was he thinking? She barely knew him.

He met the stony gazes of the guy who'd tried to protect Sariah and severe bun-lady. The guy was his first massage. He must've been standing outside the door to burst in that quickly.

Grabbing his shirt, he tugged it on and walked toward them.

They both backed out of the way. Mack felt like he should apologize to them, but he hadn't done anything wrong.

He walked quietly to the receptionist desk and pulled out his credit card. Bun-lady finally came and took it, charging him for the third massage, even though he hadn't really gotten much of a massage. He left a generous tip, gave her a forced smile, and headed outside. A brisk, spring wind hit him as he trudged to his rented Cherokee. This roller coaster with Sariah was killing him. He'd finally found her, she was flirting with him, and then, bam, he'd somehow messed it all up again. At least she'd said she'd meet him at six. He'd been terrified she'd rescind their dinner agreement.

Settling into the Cherokee, he tilted the chair back and closed his eyes, hoping he could rest and the dull headache that was starting behind his eyes would disappear.

His phone rang. He pulled it out without sitting up. "Hello," he muttered, hoping it was Navy or one of his brothers. He could really use some advice from his sister.

"Mack," the voice was unhappy and he instantly recognized it as Hyde Metcalf's voice.

He sat up and wondered if the angels in heaven were conspiring against him. "Hey, Hyde."

"Caleb called me."

"Figures."

"You found Sariah?"

"Yeah." He stared out of the windshield at the bright spring day.

The wind rustled budding tree branches. Why had he come here? Did he even have a chance with Sariah?

"And?" Hyde's voice was tight and controlled.

"She's going to dinner with me at six."

"Did you bully her into that?"

"What? Come on, Hyde," he protested. "Have you ever seen me bully anybody into anything?" Mack might be one of the toughest offensive linemen in the nation but he had never pushed his way around anywhere, besides the football field. He'd learned young that people were intimidated by his size and he'd tried extra hard to be kind and not give anyone a reason to fear him. Being bullied as a small child for his speech impediment had made him empathetic. He hated the thought that maybe he had scared Sariah because of his large build. The only other reason she would have freaked out like that was because there was something wrong with her face or neck.

There was a pause then Hyde finally admitted, "No."

"I just want to get to know her. Why are you so against me?"

Hyde blew out a breath. "It's not you. It's your fame and your family and Sariah is just delicate."

Mack swallowed, staring at the front of the massage school. Half an hour ago he'd think Hyde was being overprotective, but he'd witnessed ... something. "She was flirting with me and I pushed the hair from her face and it flipped her out."

"I bet it did."

"Did someone hurt her?" He was imagining everything from an abusive boyfriend to a traumatic accident.

"Sariah's very private and it's not my story to tell. I know you wouldn't intentionally hurt her, but please be careful with her. Please think about her and not your own desires."

Mack didn't know what to make of any of this. He wasn't some selfish brute that was going to push himself on Sariah. "I'll treat her like I would want someone to treat my sister."

"I guess that's all I could ask. I'll check in with you soon."

"Okay."

Hyde hung up the phone. Mack laid back against the seat and squeezed his eyes shut. This whole deal with Sariah was unnerving. Why was he so drawn to her and why did Hyde act like she was a fragile piece of beautiful pottery? The interactions he'd had with her showed she was witty, strong, and feisty. The only weird thing had been when he pushed at her hair and she screamed.

Frustration rolled through him and he second-guessed everything from his motivation to pursue her to everyone's overprotectiveness of her to even Sariah's mental health. He'd take her to dinner, but that might have to be the end of his Sariah quest. No matter how much he wanted to be with her, he couldn't allow her to be hurt.

Sariah made it through the last hour and a half of school, her mind replaying the way she'd reacted to Mack's gentle touch over and over again. Ah, Mack. He was a gentle giant and she was a freak-out crazy woman. How could she explain why she'd reacted like that? She still didn't want him to see her ugliness. She knew the way he was pursuing her would end soon, if it hadn't already, but she didn't want to see revulsion in his eyes. She could still remember the first time Tyler had seen her scars. He'd recoiled and then she'd been very careful to keep her hair covering her right side after that. She never let herself reflect on when Tyler's girlfriend and her brothers had been trying to drown her and then discovered her scars. They'd changed their plan and used her injury to exploit Tyler. Sariah knew it had probably saved her life but at the time she hadn't been certain she wanted to keep living.

She said goodbye to everyone and took a deep breath. When she walked out those doors she might be face to face with Mack Quinn. Making sure her hair was in place, she said a prayer and marched resolutely out front of the school. *You got this girl*, she muttered to herself.

Searching around, she didn't see Mack. Her stomach filled with a heavy sickness, like eating an entire loaf of stale bread by yourself then discovering it was moldy. He'd left and wasn't coming back. She didn't blame him, but oh, how it hurt. She'd known she shouldn't let herself fall for him, but stupidly she had.

Walking slowly toward the parking lot, she squinted at the sun glaring off of shiny vehicles. She walked past a black Jeep Cherokee and jumped when she saw there was a large person inside. Putting a hand on her heart, she took another quick look.

The man was inclined in the driver's seat, sleeping, and she recognized him.

Mack. She kept the hand on her heart. He hadn't left. He must've decided to wait in his car and had fallen asleep. She stood there, staring into his window. It was crazy that he could be so big yet so good-looking and non-threatening. His features were definitely male, strong and cut. The curly, blond hair softened him, but not as much as the blue eyes that she loved to stare into.

As if he sensed her staring, Mack's eyelashes fluttered and his eyes opened. He focused immediately on her. He smiled softly and her heart thumped faster.

Sitting up quickly, he pushed the door open and climbed out. Sariah stood her ground, not wanting him to think she was afraid of him. He probably already thought she was mentally unstable.

"I'm so sorry," he said immediately.

"No." Sariah shook her head. "That was on me. I apologize for reacting like a rabid badger." She smoothed her hair tighter around her neck.

Mack's eyes flicked to her neck and back to meet hers. "Can you tell me about it?"

Sariah's mouth went dry. "No," she squeaked out.

He studied her, moistened his lips, and then said, "Someday?"

She shrugged. She wanted to tell him yes, or joke away the whole thing, but she couldn't do either right now.

Mack studied her for a few beats then he nodded, as if accepting her crazy secrets. "Thai food?" he asked.

Sariah's shoulders lowered. "Thai food sounds delectable."

Mack smiled at her word choice. "Are you comfortable riding with me or would you like me to follow you?"

"I'd love to ride with you," she said quickly. She'd really messed this up, making him think she was afraid of him. She supposed many people would be, with his muscular frame, but she knew he was gentle and good.

He extended his hand and stared at her, his blue eyes asking her to trust him. Sariah placed her palm in his. He squeezed her hand and walked her around the Jeep, opening the passenger door. Sariah slid into the vehicle, so relieved he hadn't pushed her. She was going on a date with Mack Quinn. It would probably be a one and done, but she was going to enjoy every second of it.

CHAPTER TEN

Mack glanced around the small, dingy restaurant as the hostess seated them, set their menus down, and bowed herself away.

"Don't worry, they passed the health board," Sariah said.

"Maybe they bribed their way through, but no way this place actually passed any cleanliness tests."

Sariah laughed. "I didn't figure you for a big old wimp."

Mack was so happy she seemed comfortable with him again he would've eaten food from a street vendor in the Philippines. "Huge wimp, just ask my sister."

Sariah's gaze traveled over him. "So, all those lovely muscles are just for show?"

Mack wished he could show her exactly how tenderly he could hold her with his muscles, but he was pretty gun shy after her reaction at the school, especially with her unwillingness to explain. "For sure."

"I know that's a lie. I've watched you push around defenders like they were bitty babies."

Did that mean she was afraid of him? "Most people don't even notice the linemen, too focused on the superstars like the Rocket and Hyde."

"I don't even know who the Rocket is and Lily watched Hyde close enough for the both of us." She glanced down at her menu then back up at him. "My gaze never left the offensive line."

Mack's heart was thumping faster and faster. Everybody knew who the Rocket was. But all he cared about was Sariah was back to flirtation mode, and he loved it. Yet part of him was terrified of how taken he was by her. His mom and Navy had warned him repeatedly to stay away from women with mental health issues. They'd explained it wasn't the woman's fault, but it could sure make life miserable for a family if the wife and mother was unstable. His mind was racing ahead though, he'd barely gotten Sariah to come to dinner with him. He couldn't be worrying about her being his other half, and how that might affect their future children. Children? It was really hot in here.

"You are ready to order?" a small Oriental lady was at his elbow.

"Um ..." Mack looked to Sariah.

"Do you trust me?" she asked.

The question hit him hard, especially as she searched his eyes with her dark brown gaze. He did. Maybe he was a fool for it, but he trusted her with so much more than his dinner order in this hole-in-the-wall restaurant. "Yes," he said.

Sariah's eyes were serious for half a second then she grinned and turned to the lady. "We'll have the pineapple fried rice, the pad thai, the papaya salad, cashew nut chicken, the red curry, oh, and the mango sticky rice."

"Ah, yes. All the entrees you like spicy?" the lady pumped her eyebrows at Mack.

"Sure." He shrugged.

"A three," Sariah said. "He looks big but he's too tender to stomach a five."

The lady laughed, took their menus, and bustled off. A young girl brought them waters. Mack thought it was interesting they hadn't even asked if they wanted a different drink.

"I'm tender?" he asked.

"Don't even try to deny it."

"Does that mean you aren't afraid of me?"

"Why would I be ...?" Her eyes lit with understanding. "I'm not afraid of you, Mack."

"That means a lot to me."

"How could I be afraid when I know you're a big old wimp off the field?" She grinned to show she was teasing.

Mack felt relief rush through him. She wasn't afraid and she knew he had a tender side. He reached out and put his hand over hers. "All right, you can tease me and call me 'a big old wimp' and make me eat at questionable restaurants, as long as you promise to spend tomorrow with me."

Sariah turned her hand over and linked their fingers. "I'd love to, but I have school."

"On a Saturday?"

She nodded. "Sunday and Monday are our days off. Lots of massage clients come in on Saturdays."

"I'd say I'd come back for a massage tomorrow, but I don't know how welcome I am there."

She released his hand and tucked her hair around the right side of her neck then toyed with her water glass. "Yeah. I'm sorry."

"No, I shouldn't have brought it up again." But he really, really wished he knew what had happened, especially now that she'd said she wasn't afraid of him. He wanted to see past her hair, see if there was something wrong, but he wondered if it wasn't more likely that some guy had scared her. That was the feeling he got from Hyde, and from everybody else who was overprotective of her. "But you'll go out with me tomorrow night?"

She took a sip of her water and then gave him a mischievous grin, the teasing Sariah restored. "I don't know, Mack Quinn. You're counting your chickens before they've even been put in the incubator."

He grinned. His knowledge of raising chickens was sadly lacking. "I'm hoping they don't feed us a raw chicken in this place."

"Oh! You are going to eat those words. An hour from now you'll be begging my forgiveness for dissing on my spot and planning when you can come back. You'll have dreams about this food."

Mack would have dreams about her, but he doubted he'd dream about this food. "We'll see," was all he said. He didn't care what the food tasted like, or if they were in violation of health codes. He was finally with Sariah. Maybe there was something wrong with her physically or mentally but he didn't care. He was finally getting his chance to get to know her.

***

Sariah appreciated the easy flow of conversation with Mack as they ate the delicious food. He'd told her a little bit about his large family, explaining the connection of Scarlett Lily to his brother Griff. She appreciated hearing the truth of that interaction from his lips. Occasionally he looked searchingly at her, probably wishing she'd tell him why she acted so crazy at the school, but he didn't ask again.

She'd ordered a lot of food, assuming that he could eat a lot, and he had proven her right. His manners were impeccable, and he made sure she always got first chance at a dish, but when she assured him several times that she was full, he cleaned off each plate.

"You ready to eat crow, my boy?" she asked as he ate the last noodle from the pad thai plate and she finished off the last bite of mango sticky rice. The coconut sauce was delicious.

He nodded. "I'm thinking of ordering some to take back to the hotel."

She punched a fist in the air. "Yes! I knew I'd win this battle. I'm more battle savvy than Napoleon."

Mack covered her hand with his own and she had to keep her head on straight as her body reacted to his simple touch.

"You'd win any battle with me," he said.

Sariah gave him a sassy smile when she wanted to tell him her every secret and beg him to move to Colorado. "I hope I never have a battle with you."

Mack studied her. "Will you go to dinner with me tomorrow night?"

"I wouldn't miss it."

His smile made her stomach heat up.

"Big guy like the food?" their waitress asked.

"Very much. Can I get a pad thai to go? Level four heat. And another order of mango sticky rice." He handed over a credit card. "Would you like any dessert or something else?" he asked Sariah before the woman left.

"No, thank you." She couldn't believe he had really ordered more food. Midnight snack? As strong as he was it probably took quite a bit of calories to maintain his muscle mass.

They chatted some more about their large families as they waited for the to-go order and then walked out to his rental. The ride back to the school parking lot passed too quickly and before she knew it, Sariah was standing outside her beat-up Civic staring up at Mack. The evening was cold but she hardly felt it as his warm gaze lingered on her.

"Thank you for an absolutely lovely dinner," she said.

"Everything with you is a little sarcastic, isn't it?"

"Ah," she protested. "That was sincere through and through." Sarcasm had protected her many a time and was pretty much the only weapon in her arsenal.

He chuckled and rested one hand against the hood of the car, leaning closer to her but not touching her. Sariah's insides did a happy jig and she leaned a little closer as well. She doubted he'd kiss her, especially after her reaction earlier today, but he'd flown clear across the country and he'd said a man didn't do that unless he wanted a kiss. Hopefully, that meant he'd try to pull her close again, this time without touching the right side of her face.

"Thank you for dinner," she said breathily.

He nodded, his blue eyes giving her this beautiful smoldering look as he leaned even closer.

"Wowzers," she mumbled.

"What?"

"I never knew real people could do that."

"Do what?"

"That smoldering, *I'm going to lean close and schmooze you with my beautiful blue eyes,* like off a movie screen." Her face got hot. She shouldn't have said any of that, but she had to break the tension somehow.

He smiled as if he thought she was hilarious, but possibly a little unstable. "I'm guessing the smoldering look didn't work if you're making fun of me."

"Oh, no, it's working." She gave in to the longings she'd had since the first time she'd seen him, all burly and tough in his football uniform, and placed both palms on his chest. "Whoa. Those muscles are ... tantalizing."

Mack gave her a soft chuckle. "Are you ever serious about anything?"

"No, not really."

"Would you ever be serious about me?"

"Doubtful you'll stay around that long." Her heart was beating so fast. She knew this couldn't last. Eventually he'd see her deformity and he'd be repulsed by her, or best-case scenario, pity her. Worst case, the media would catch wind of them and somehow expose her, like they had four years ago when Tyler's other girlfriend took all those pictures and told so many lies to the media about her and Tyler, hoping to damage his political aspirations and destroy her life. Luckily it didn't get much attention outside of Colorado but what if Mack somehow saw those pics? They were still online.

Mack bent closer and softly brushed his lips across her cheek. Sariah's entire body heated up and all worries pushed to the background. Staying right in her space, he said, "You have no clue of the tenacity of an offensive lineman."

He straightened, opened her door, and waited for her to slip inside. "Six o'clock tomorrow, here?" he said, as if he hadn't just upended her world by the simple touch of his lips, and made it impossible for her to sleep tonight.

She nodded.

"Can't wait." He shut the door, gave her one more grin, and sauntered to the Cherokee.

Sariah wilted against the seat, her eyes feasting on all those muscles working in synchrony. Being this close to him was better than watching him play football, and that was really saying something.

CHAPTER ELEVEN

Mack got a suite at the Four Seasons Hotel in downtown Denver. He slept late the next morning then worked out for a couple of hours in the gym and ate breakfast before showering, getting his rental from the valet, and driving around Denver aimlessly. He found himself driving west and then up the mountain back to Sariah's hometown of Georgetown. He wanted to go see her little brother, Josh, again but thought that might be too much. He contented himself with grabbing a couple of sandwiches at the Mountain Buzz Café then driving up the mountain pass. He stopped at a turnout that turned out to be a trailhead and went on a hike through the trees and along a creek. It was chilly outside and he felt awake and energized by it.

When he made it back to the Cherokee it was late afternoon. Only a few more hours until he could pick up Sariah. He drove I-70 for a while, simply enjoying the views of the mountains and then he headed back. As he left the towering mountains and headed east to Denver, his phone rang.

He pushed the button on the steering wheel. "Hello?"

"My favorite brother."

"Navy! How'd you know I've been wanting to talk to you?"

She laughed. "Because you always want to talk to me. How's life?"

"Great, but I need some womanly advice."

"Whoa. That sounds intense, lucky for you I'm the woman to give it. What's up?"

Mack stayed with the flow of traffic as he chatted. "I met someone."

"Excuse me?" Navy sounded confused but Mack knew it was all a ploy. "You can't date, you're only like twelve-years-old."

"Ha, ha. Try twenty-five, sis."

"You blink and they grow up." She gave a dramatic sigh. "Is this a serious met someone or is it like a Colt, *I meet someone perfect every week*, kind of deal?"

"It's pretty serious."

"Are you going to be following Ryder and Kaleb's example into marital bliss?"

"Okay, not that serious." Not that he was opposed to marriage or marrying Sariah, but he wasn't one to rush into things. "What about you?"

She tsked her tongue. "Not talking about me and you know Colt's too much of a player to get married and Griff's too grumpy. So, I guess it is time for you. Mama needs grandbabies and all that business."

"Does Mama give you a hard time about not giving her grandbabies?" The hurt in Navy's voice came clearly through the line.

"Always, but once again, this isn't about me. What's her name and how'd you meet her?"

Mack changed lanes to let the Nissan riding inches off his bumper get around. "She came to my games all season, I got brave enough to talk to her after a couple of them. Then at the party celebrating the Super Bowl win we connected again. I couldn't stop thinking about her so I had Griff track her down. By the way, did you know Griff dated Scarlett Lily in college?"

"No, and that is fabulous info to have, thank you." Mack could just hear his sister's brain clicking the info in to torment Griff later. He probably shouldn't have shared it. "So, you found this mystery woman?"

"Yes. She lives near Denver. I took her to dinner last night. She's amazing, sis."

"But ..." She drawled it out.

"There's no but."

"There is definitely a but. I know you, I know your buts in all forms. I changed your diapers for crying out loud. Tell me about the but."

Mack laughed softly but this was why he wanted to talk to Navy.

"She hides the right side of her face and neck with her hair. It's really odd. I almost pushed the hair back yesterday and she freaked."

He took the exit for Sariah's school. It was close to six now.

"That is a little disturbing. So, what's your question?"

"I just don't know how to proceed. I don't mind being chill and waiting for her to share her secrets with me, but what if there's something really off with her mentally and I should ease back before I'm too invested?" The problem was he was already too invested and even though Sariah's reaction had been intense he didn't feel like she was crazy or anything.

"Why don't you have Griff research her?"

"He told me 'no more'," he imitated Griff's gruff voice, "after he helped me track her down, and I just don't feel right about it. It's her secret to tell, right?"

"Hmm. I guess you could look at it like that, or you could Google her and see what you find."

Mack had thought about it, but he wanted to earn her trust and have her tell him ... whatever secrets she had. "Yeah, I don't think so. Hopefully, she'll tell me about it soon."

"So you're camping out in Denver until she succumbs to your oversized charm?"

"The idea has crossed my mind." He had to be back in Atlanta Monday morning, but he would fly here every weekend, if Sariah wanted him to.

"You are almost as sappy as Kaleb, you know that, right? At least he has Jasmine now to keep him in line. Will this girl sass you as good as Mama or I?"

"I think she could."

"Oh, good. She might stand a chance with our family."

"Do you think I'm crazy to pursue her this hard?"

"I think she's crazy if she resists you. You're the best guy I know, Mack. And I know a lot of guys."

"Thanks, sis." His sister and mama were tough, but they loved him and thought the world of him. He needed that right now as he was uncertain how to proceed with Sariah, but knew he couldn't pass up spending more time with her.

"Tell me more about the Scarlett Lily thing."

Mack smiled but regretted saying anything. Mack might be big, muscular, and intimidating to ninety-nine percent of the population, but Griff could still thump him. Griff was the toughest man he knew, and his brother had helped him find Sariah so he owed him.

He recounted the story quick, though, because he never told Navy no, but his mind was already wandering ahead. Less than ten minutes and he'd see Sariah again.

Sariah got done a few minutes early and hurried to the parking lot, hoping to see Mack's rented Cherokee waiting there. She grinned when she spotted it and hurried over. Mack had his phone to his ear, causing her to stop abruptly rather than rip his door open and hug him because she was so happy to see him.

He noticed her, gave her a big grin, and swung his door open. "Love you. See you soon." He climbed out of the Jeep, pushed end on the phone, then dropped it in his pocket. "Hey. How was school?"

Sariah envisioned him meeting her every day after school. She thought that would be just about perfect, but she needed to know something and quick. A shot of terror raced through her. "Love you?" She planted her hands on her hips and stared pointedly up at him. "Please tell me that was your mama or your sister."

His grin grew. "Do I detect some jealousy, Miss Udy?"

"No, sir. But I am only party to monogamous relationships." He had no clue how serious she was about this, but if he was already two-timing her he wouldn't have let her hear the "love you", right? Tyler had been amazing at keeping his girlfriends separate and oblivious to each other's existence, until Denise somehow found out about Sariah and then tracked her down.

Mack chuckled and took a step closer, reaching out his large hand. Sariah couldn't stop herself from putting her hand in his. It was a brisk spring evening and her hands were chilly. Mack's hand around hers immediately warmed her hand and the smile on his face thawed her from the inside out. "So, you're saying we have a relationship?" he asked in his melodious voice.

"Whoa, back it right up, boy. I said nothing about 'having' a relationship. But I might be open to the *possibility* of a relationship, in the future, not immediate future, but maybe not too far in the future future, if, and only if, you tell me who you just said love you to."

"Wow. That was a whole lot of confusing lingo and I'm just a simple offensive lineman." He arched one eyebrow, looking so handsome and doing that beautiful, *I will gaze at you until you beg me to kiss you,* thing with his eyes. "Do we have a relationship then?"

She laughed, though she was still churning inside with worry over that love you, and pushed at his shoulder with her free hand. Of course, he didn't budge, but it was fun to touch his muscular shoulder. "You're about as simple as Killer Sudoku."

"Killer Sudoku?" He grinned.

"Tougher than regular Sudoku. I fail at it regularly and my teachers claimed I was good at math. What I'm saying is there's nothing simple about you. The answer to your question is, if you're a patient man, maybe. What's the answer to mine?"

"I am pretty patient." He squeezed her hand and admitted, "My sister."

"Finally, he answers my question. And they say women talk in circles." She prayed it truly was his sister. Part of her wanted to keep grilling him, simply because she hadn't trusted an un-related man in the past four years, she'd acted crazy enough yesterday and she hated to scare him completely away.

Mack arched an eyebrow. "You're claiming that whole spiel about relationships wasn't talking in circles?"

Sariah giggled. She had never had so much fun bantering with someone. "Where are we eating?"

He shook his head, led her around the vehicle, and opened her door. "You're the local, and I actually didn't get food poisoning last night. Where do you suggest?"

"Ha, ha."

He grinned, shut her door, and hurried around the front of the vehicle. She loved watching him move. Depending on how late he took her home tonight, she was going to watch highlights of him on YouTube. He climbed in and the vehicle rocked slightly. It was amazing he could be so massive yet so fit and appealing.

"Where to?" he asked.

"Hmm. Do you like Indian food?"

He shrugged. "Honestly, Sariah, do you think I got to this size not liking every kind of food?"

She giggled at that. "Valid reasoning." She pointed. "Great Indian restaurant just a few blocks that a way."

He put the vehicle into gear.

"It looks really good on you."

He glanced over at her. "What does?"

"Your size."

"Thank you." He smiled as he navigated to the restaurant.

They walked inside and the hostess seated them at a small corner table with a clean but scratched wooden top. Mack glanced around. "It looks a little less sketchy than last night. And it smells good."

"Well, thank you for the approval. I aim to tantalize."

Mack's eyes widened and then a slow smile grew on his handsome face. "Yes, you do."

"I meant ... your taste buds." Wow, she wasn't making this any better.

His voice got low and husky. "I look forward to it."

"Stop." She pushed at his arm, her face filling with heat.

"I don't think I'm the one who started this."

The waitress interrupted, bringing them waters and asking if they wanted anything different than water to drink. They both declined. "Are you ready to order?"

Mack nodded to Sariah. "Will you order for us again?"

She smiled. "I don't want you going away hungry. Should I order more than last night?"

"Please."

She could definitely get used to this. She'd felt guilty last night when she'd gotten home late but Teresa had demanded all the details of her date and made her promise she'd go again tonight. Lily and Hyde were with Teresa tonight and would be through Sunday night. Hyde hadn't said much about her going out with Mack, but he seemed very concerned for her. Lily had obviously told him too much about the Tyler fiasco. She focused back on the menu.

"Let's do the alu gobi, tandori chicken, beef vindaloo, butter chicken, chana masala, chickpea curry, and we'd better have some spring rolls." She glanced at Mack. "Is that enough food?"

"We'll see."

Sariah laughed and handed the menu back. "Thank you."

"I'll bring the spring rolls soon." She took their menus and walked away.

Sariah took a drink of her water.

"You like *tantalizing* exotic foods the best?" Mack asked.

"Definitely."

"Have you always?"

She picked at the edge of the paper tablecloth. "My family doesn't have a lot of ... money. So, our diet growing up was pretty simple." She forced a smile and met his eyes. "Usually fish or deer for our meat that my dad had caught or hunted, potatoes and carrots for our veggies, and my mom made loaves and loaves of bread and raspberry jam to keep everybody filled up."

Mack swallowed. "I'm sorry."

"No." She waved a hand. "I had a great childhood and I love my family. I was just explaining. Last year I started working for Hyde, taking care of Teresa. For the first time in my life I had extra money and I was here in Denver so I tried out different foods and I found I loved them."

"I like that you're adventurous."

She couldn't meet his gaze now. The only adventurous things she ever did were try out new foods and go on hikes in the mountains, or maybe swim in the lake in the summer. Her life was so boring. What made her think she could keep a man like Mack Quinn interested in her? She quickly changed the subject, "So tell me more about your family. Your sister, Navy, is the oldest? She's so tough, like my sister, Lily. I love that."

He smiled. "She is tough, and not just fitness wise. She can put any of us in our place, even Griff."

"Griff's the Navy SEAL, right?" Like she'd forget Griff. He was the reason Scarlett Lily had kissed Mack, but she didn't want to look like a stalker.

He nodded. "You know a lot about my family."

"I do have WiFi and Google. Does that bother you that so many people know about you?"

He shrugged. "Comes with the territory playing football and everybody in my family seems to have found their way to a visible career, except for Griff and Colt. Griff says the world quietly. Colt's visible because he's always dating somebody famous."

"I did notice that. You all look a lot alike too."

He stared at her for a beat. "What would you do if I Googled you?"

Sariah's throat tightened and she tugged at the hair covering her neck. Mack's gaze became more tender. He knew something was wrong with her. He was too kind to come out and ask her about it though. "You haven't?"

His gaze was clear and steady. "No, I haven't."

"Please don't," she murmured.

He studied her before nodding. "I won't."

"Thank you." The relief was strong but could she trust him? She didn't know Mack that well and already she had to trust that the person he'd said "love you" to was his sister and that he wouldn't Google her. She hadn't Googled herself for a long time, but could only imagine the horrific pictures and accusations would still be there.

Luckily the waitress brought their spring rolls right then. The food was delicious, but they never regained the carefree conversation.

Mack walked Sariah to her car after dinner, not sure how to restore the easiness that had been between them, before he asked her if he could Google her. Dumb, dumb, dumb. He knew she was sensitive about something. So, whatever was going on with her, there was a record, probably pictures, of it online. That made him crazy with interest, but he'd told her he wouldn't look, so he wouldn't.

He swung open her door. She smiled up at him. "Thank you for dinner."

"Sure."

She bit at her lip and then asked, "Will I see you again?"

"Do you want to?" He shouldn't have asked it like that, but he wasn't sure how to proceed with her and not hit a sensitive button again.

She looked so beautiful as she blinked up at him. "Mack ... I haven't dated anyone in four years."

The confusion must've been evident on his face, because she smiled and looked away. "I haven't."

"But why?" Obviously, it had something to do with whatever she was hiding, or what she'd been through, but he couldn't imagine men didn't hit on her nonstop. "You're gorgeous and funny and smart and ... do you just tell every man no?"

She focused back on him and nodded. "Yes, I do."

"Why me?"

"There's something about you that I could never say no to." She grasped his shoulders, lifted herself onto tiptoes, and kissed his cheek.

Mack savored the softness of her lips against him and the sweetness of her scent. It was an appealing mix of vanilla and musk. He about grabbed her and pulled her in for a real kiss but she slipped into her car. He grasped the door. "So, you're saying you want to date me?"

"I'm saying I'm interested in a *monogamous* relationship with a huge, studly offensive lineman," she said. "Yes, I want to date you."

Yes! He almost punched a fist in the air. Whatever odd thing was going on with her, it didn't matter to him. He wanted more time with her. Once she knew him better she'd tell him about it. "I have to fly back home tomorrow night for a meeting with some sponsors Monday morning. Can I be with you tomorrow?" he rushed out.

"Are you a church-goer?"

"Yes, ma'am."

"Meet me at the First Presbyterian Church of Georgetown, Colorado at precisely ten a.m."

He grinned. "I will be there."

"Plan on dinner with the family after. It'll probably be fish."

He laughed. "I like fish."

"You like everything." She blinked up at him and he wanted to tug her back out of the car and kiss her, but she hadn't dated anyone in four years. She was probably only twenty-one or twenty-two, so basically, she hadn't dated since high school. Crazy. She had an interesting story and he wanted to know it, but mostly he wanted to do this right and take it slow and be with her.

"I mostly just like you," he said.

She put a hand to her heart. "You're a charmer, Mack Quinn, I don't care what they say about you."

He chuckled and only a lot of self-control allowed him to say, "I'll see you tomorrow," and close her door. He watched her drive away. And he cursed himself for promising not to Google her.

CHAPTER TWELVE

Sariah sat in the hard pews, with Josh on her right side, wondering if Mack was going to show. Her family usually tried to squish in one row near the back of the chapel, but Hyde, Lily, and Teresa were here today and Sariah had been forced to admit to everyone that Mack was coming, so she could save him a spot. She checked the entry one more time—empty. She glanced at her phone—ten a.m. on the dot. The gaping open spot to her left probably confused her fellow church-goers. Sariah had never brought anyone to church.

Hyde leaned across Josh, put both hands over Josh's ears and muttered, "If he breaks your heart, I'm going to rip him apart."

"Good luck with that one," she said.

"I don't care how big he is, you haven't seen me mad."

"I've seen you psychotic, like right now, and it doesn't look good on you." Usually she loved her surrogate big brother, but she didn't need to be reminded that she'd been stood up. It hurt enough.

Hyde gave her a tight smile. "You just wait and you'll see psychotic. I'm not putting up with him hurting you when I warned him."

Josh squirmed and looked up at Hyde. "Why you covering my ears?" he said, very loudly, just as the pastor stood at the pulpit.

Several people turned around. Josh lifted his hands, all innocence. He was so cute the people just smiled and turned back around.

Hyde gave her one more concerned look. Sariah loved Hyde, but he must not know Mack very well. Mack wouldn't hurt her. She discreetly checked over her shoulder. The door remained stubbornly closed. At least not intentionally. At least she didn't think so. She sighed. What did she know? She'd trusted Tyler the two-timer. They'd dated for six months and she'd never seen through his lies.

The church door whooshed open and Sariah whipped around to look. Mack walked in. She'd seen him in a suit the night of the Patriots' party. Seeing him in a suit for the second time was just as delicious as the first. The perfectly-tailored navy blue suit complimented his muscular, broad frame. His blue eyes sparkled at her and his blond curls were gelled and smoothed away from his handsome face.

"Mack Quinn is at my church!" Josh was so excited he yelled, interrupting the pastor's opening remarks.

"Shh," Mary and Trudy said together.

Sariah just stared at Mack as he eased in next to her. He reached his arm around her shoulder and whispered into her left ear, "Sorry for being late. An accident blocked the freeway."

"It's okay." He was here. She wanted to jump up and cheer.

The congregation was buzzing. They'd gotten used to seeing Hyde Metcalf over the past year but to have another Patriots' football player coming to church with the Udy family must've pushed them right over the edge. Especially since it was Sariah he had his arm around.

The pastor cleared his throat but the chatting continued. Sariah ignored it as she stared up at Mack. His gaze was solely focused on her as well. "You're beautiful," he murmured.

Her cheeks heated up but she fired right back, "Not as beautiful as you."

Josh climbed onto her lap. "Can I sit by you, Mr. Quinn?" he asked, all innocent and cute.

Sariah didn't want to be displaced from Mack's side, but she would do anything for Josh. Mack easily solved the dilemma by unwrapping his arm from Sariah's shoulder, plucking Josh off her lap and onto his left leg. He was so big that was all the space Josh needed.

Josh grinned. "You're so tough," he said, very loudly.

Sariah laughed. She glanced up and most of the congregation was crane-necking.

"We'd like to welcome Mack Quinn to our congregation today," the pastor said. "Can we please proceed with the prayer now?"

People whipped back around. Mack kept his left arm around Josh but wrapped his right around Sariah again. She settled into his side and didn't know when church had been so exciting, or comfortable. Mack was a great mixture of both for her. As soon as the prayer ended, Josh started whispering excitedly in Mack's ear. Mack responded to her little brother, even as he pulled Sariah tighter against his chest and abdomen. A thrill shot through her. The pastor's words, everyone's interested glances, and Hyde's concerned looks all went over her head. The only thing she could focus on was Mack Quinn.

M ack felt like a giant in the small dining room of the Udy home. He'd enjoyed church, whispering with Josh and holding Sariah close. Maybe he'd moved too fast, keeping his arm around her throughout the meeting, but only Hyde seemed to be giving him the stink eye. Her parents, family, and the rest of the congregation welcomed him openly. He met so many people after church he couldn't begin to remember any of their names. Luckily, he had Sariah's family down.

Mack had helped peel and chop potatoes on the back patio table with Josh before dinner while everyone else did "more important jobs" in Josh's words. He loved being around Sariah's little brother. The little guy was full of excitement and football trivia and seemed to idolize Mack, almost as much as Hyde.

Now everyone was squished around the large dining room table, passing food and chatting. Josh had made sure he was sitting between Mack and Hyde. Sariah was on Mack's right side with Josh on his left. She seemed a lot more comfortable with him on her left so he tried to stay on that side whenever he could.

There were several conversations going on so Mack felt comfortable to just ladle food onto his plate, eat, and observe. There was a lot of food—trout, a venison roast, mashed potatoes and gravy, corn, green beans, and homemade rolls—and it all tasted good. Mack was grateful that the family seemed to have plenty of food and they all dressed nice. The house was small and worn, but it was clean and he felt love here just like at his parents' home in Rhode Island.

"Mr. Quinn, sir," Josh said through a mouthful of potatoes, "do you think the Rocket and Hyde can take you to the Super Bowl again next year? Hyde won't promise me anything."

Mack smiled at Hyde over Josh's head. He'd always liked Hyde and hoped they could get past this weird vibe of Hyde trying to protect Sariah from Mack. In fairness to Hyde, Mack hadn't heeded his warnings, but how could Mack have stayed away from Sariah?

Hyde gave him a tentative smile back and ruffled Josh's hair. "I keep telling you, bud, if I promise and it doesn't happen that makes me a liar."

Josh wrinkled his nose. "Then just make it happen!" He shoved a bite of roll dripping with jam into his mouth and said around the bite, "Right, Mr. Quinn?"

"First of all, it's Mack."

"Oh, good luck with that one," Hyde said. "It took me months to get him to call me Hyde."

Everyone laughed at that and Lily said, "You're his idol, give the kid a break."

"I'd better be your idol," Hyde said, leaning down and kissing her.

"Stop that," Caleb groaned, but they were all smiling.

Lily whispered something only for Hyde's ears.

Mack met Sariah's gaze, wishing he dared kiss her, but he wouldn't be doing it in front of her family.

Josh tugged on his sleeve. "I'm serious, Mr. Quinn, sir. If you promise me, I know nobody can get through you to the Rocket and then the Rocket will have all kinds of time to get the ball to Hyde, and you know Hyde is the best receiver in the world! How can you not make the Super Bowl?"

Mack loved this kid, but he agreed with Hyde. The Super Bowl wasn't something any team could guarantee. "We will try our very best, Josh."

Josh sighed and mopped up some gravy with a chunk of roll. "I guess that's all I can ask of you, Mr. Quinn."

"I can ask you to call me Mack."

Josh looked up at him. "Okay, sir, I'll call you Mack. If you bring your brother, Kaleb Quinn here to meet me. He's the best singer in the world!"

Mack laughed and the conversation shifted to talking about Kaleb and Jasmine and then everyone wanted him to recount the story of being kidnapped last spring. The dinner and afternoon were pleasant and Mack felt accepted and comfortable with her family. But he really wanted to get Sariah alone again.

CHAPTER THIRTEEN

Sariah thought dinner and hanging out after dinner went well. Hyde seemed to calm down and Josh and the rest of her siblings made the conversation fun and interesting. The time went too fast before Mack was saying, "I have to make a five o'clock flight."

Sariah's stomach and neck tightened. He was leaving. Would he want to come back? He'd said last night that he liked her and wanted to date her but the fact remained that he lived across the nation and she wasn't going to be flying to Atlanta anytime soon with her school schedule and job of being with Teresa. She had more money than she'd ever had with Hyde paying her much too generously for being his mom's companion and she didn't want to mess that up. She knew Hyde had also paid off her parents' home and set up education funds for each of them, but her dad wouldn't allow any more generosity than that.

She stood and watched as Mack said goodbye to everyone then she started toward the door with him.

"Why don't I walk Mack out?" Hyde said suddenly.

Sariah whirled and glared at him. "Over my incapacitated body."

Everyone started laughing and Lily tugged Hyde back onto the couch by her. "She's okay," Lily said quietly.

Sariah's dad was giving Hyde odd looks, probably wondering why he was taking over his role.

"Thank you for dinner," Mack said again to her mom. "It was delicious."

"Thank you for being here," her mom said.

Her dad walked with them to the door, shook Mack's hand and said goodbye. Sariah wondered if he was bugged by Hyde trying to act like he was the father figure.

Finally, they were outside and alone. It was a chilly spring day. She hugged herself for warmth. Mack's arm came around her and with his large body sheltering her from the wind, she was much warmer. He escorted her around his Jeep where it might be possible her family couldn't see them. She wouldn't put anything past her family though. Brandon had probably rigged a drone to video them from the sky. She glanced around but didn't see anything.

Mack stopped and wrapped both arms around her, simply holding her close. Awareness shot through her. He was so tough and appealing to her.

"Thank you for letting me be with you this weekend," Mack said.

Sariah tilted her head up to look into his blue eyes. "Thanks for tracking me to the ends of the earth."

He chuckled. "I would've, you know?"

She bit at her lip. "So now that you've found me, and gotten to know me a little bit, was it worth it to be more persistent than Colonel Sanders?"

"Colonel Sanders?" His brow wrinkled.

"He was rejected by 1009 restaurants before one agreed to his ideas."

Mack's throaty chuckle made her silliness all worth it, but then his gaze deepened. "You could reject me 1009 times and I'd keep coming back."

Sariah's heart leapt. The man for her would have to be persistent, but would Mack truly be that persistent? "So all your effort to find me was worth it?" she asked again.

"I don't know yet." There was a teasing glint in his blue eyes.

"Aw!" Sariah tried to pull back out of his arms but he held her tight. "So, when are you going to know?"

"After you kiss me."

The words were said bravely but Sariah could tell they hadn't rolled off his tongue. "How long have you been planning that line?" she asked.

"Since the first time I saw you."

His blue gaze seared through her as he pulled her onto her tiptoes and bent down close. Sariah's breath was coming in short pants and the cool spring air was suddenly blazing hot. She wrapped her hands around his broad shoulders, reveling in the muscle underneath her fingertips.

"What are you waiting for then?" she asked, her voice shaky.

Mack grinned slightly. "Our audience to disappear." He tilted his head toward the front of her house. Through the Jeep's windows her siblings pressed against the living room window were quite a sight.

Sariah sighed, knowing they wouldn't be going away any time soon.

Mack chuckled, swept her off her feet and cradled her against his chest. Sariah gasped for air, clinging to his neck for stability.

"This isn't going to get them to go away."

"No," he agreed, "But this will make it so they can't see us." With her still in his arms he knelt on the gravel drive and then spun around onto his rear and leaned against the vehicle.

Sariah leaned into him. "You'll ruin your suit."

"I have other suits." He focused on her lips and murmured, "But this is the first time I've gotten brave enough to kiss Sariah Udy."

Sariah could hardly think straight, let alone catch a breath. He smelled like his delicious sandalwood cologne and he looked even better. She ran her fingers up his neck and entangled them in his short curls. "Well then, you'd better not miss it."

Mack smiled and his lips finally met hers. Warmth and joy rushed through her as he tenderly kissed her. There was nothing demanding about this kiss, it was as if he was savoring the connection rather than trying to passionately claim her, but there was still plenty of passion and sparks swirling between them. Mack's hands were safely around her waist so she didn't have to worry about him touching her neck or scars.

The kiss wasn't long, but it still overwhelmed her senses. Mack tasted like her mom's blueberry cobbler, his lips were soft and warm, and his body was hard and surrounded hers as if he would not only keep her warm, but protect her from every future harm or worry.

He pulled back and rested his forehead against hers. No words were needed between them and for once Sariah didn't want to give a smart-alecky quip. She simply wanted to stare into Mack's blue eyes and have his muscular arms hold her close.

The front door opened and his head swiveled toward the sound. Josh came around the back of the vehicle. "What are you two *doing?*" he demanded.

Mack chuckled and Sariah buried her head in his chest. He lifted her onto her feet and stood quickly beside her. "I'm just telling your sister goodbye."

Josh's eyebrows lifted. "Well, don't do it on the ground." He looked at Sariah. "Mom and Dad wondered if you were okay and asked me to come check." His eyes widened, *"But* I wasn't supposed to tell you that."

Smart. Send the innocent little boy to check on them. "I'm

good." She looked up at Mack. "I'm as good as Mom's blueberry cobbler."

Mack's gaze was full of her. "You taste better," he whispered.

"That's weird," Josh said.

"I'm coming in now," Sariah said, though she didn't want to let Mack leave. This weekend had been magical for her and she wanted it to continue.

"Bye, Mr. Quinn, sir."

"Uh-uh, you said you'd call me Mack."

Josh's dark eyes filled with a mischievous light. "I said if you brought Kaleb Quinn to meet me, I'd call you Mack."

"Josh!" Sariah shook her head. "Stop being so conniving." She looked up at Mack. "You know what the baby of the family is like."

Mack simply smiled. "I know all about being the youngest." He moved quick, darting to Josh, picking him off the ground, and tossing him in the air like he was a baby.

Josh howled with delight. When Mack caught him, he gave him a quick squeeze and said, "We'll see what we can do about you meeting Kaleb. Can you please call me Mack?"

"Yes, sir, Mack sir."

Mack chuckled at him and then set him on the ground. "I'll see you soon, bud."

"Bye, Mack." Josh ran back into the house, slamming the door behind him.

Sariah checked and everybody was still unfortunately pressed against the window. She focused back on Mack.

"I guess I'd better go before they send somebody else to check on us." He smiled but he also pulled open the driver's side door. She didn't want him to go. She wanted to spend every minute with him. She had vacation days from school she'd never used. What if ... No. She wasn't brave enough to suggest she take days off school so she could stay with him twenty-four hours.

"Mack."

He glanced over at her. "Yeah?"

"Am I going to see you again?"

He gave her a slow grin. "You thought you were getting rid of me that easily?"

She bit at her lip. "Not if I'm a lucky duck."

He lifted his right hand and brushed his fingers down the left side of her face. "I've worked far too hard to find you, Sariah Udy. No way I'm giving up now."

"So, it's all about the pursuit. Not that you really want to be with the most hilarious woman I know." She put her hands on her hips, hoping he didn't realize she was also the most insecure woman she knew.

Mack chuckled. "You are hilarious and this has nothing to do with the pursuit. It's all about me wanting to be with you." He bent forward and gently kissed her then he pulled back and said, "You have my number?"

She nodded. Teresa and Allie had made sure of that.

"Will you text me, please?"

"I'll flip a coin. You want heads or tails?"

He grinned. "No coins. I can't leave this one to chance."

"Life's a gamble." She shrugged innocently.

He stepped closer, his strong body brushing hers. "If you don't text me, I'll be waiting at the school Saturday at six o'clock."

"If I do reveal the rock star I am and text you, you'd better be waiting at the school *every* day at six o'clock."

"Every day spent with Sariah Udy." He groaned, wrapped his hands around her lower back, and pulled her in close. "You have no idea how much I want to do that," he murmured against her left cheek.

"Then why don't you?" She was being all kinds of brave. What if she chased him away? She had no clue how relationships worked.

He looked down at her, so serious it scared her a little bit. "Sariah," he said gently. "We both know there's something you're not telling me." His eyes flickered to the right side of her face and neck and back up.

Her chest tightened and terror rushed through her as all desire to tease with him splashed out like Josh had dropped another milk jug. It was not only going to make a mess it was going to curdle and reek. He wanted to see her scars, know what happened to her. Did she tell him about Tyler too? Was she ready for any of that? What if Mack saw her deformity, left her, and never returned?

"I don't want you to tell me until you're comfortable with me, until you know you can trust me."

Sariah gulped, her worries changing to surprise. He was letting her off the hook. Asking her to learn to trust him. She didn't know if she could ever trust a man, after what Tyler had done to her.

"I want to take this slow, and if I'm waiting at the school for you every day ..." He shook his head. "I'll push ahead too fast and maybe scare you away."

Sariah buried the left side of her face against his chest. Could it be possible he was really this perfect for her? He wanted to take it slow. He wanted her to trust him.

"Thank you," she managed to squeak out. Pulling back from his embrace, she gave him a watery smile, praying she wouldn't break down in front of him. "You'd better go catch that plane."

He nodded. "I'll see you Saturday."

"I'll be texting you before then."

He grinned, climbed into his vehicle, and shut the door. Sariah stepped back. He slowly reversed and with one last wave, he pulled away from the house. She watched him drive around the park and then up the road before he disappeared from sight.

"You okay?"

Sariah jumped. She whirled to see her entire family standing there. Lily was watching her with understanding but worry in her eyes.

"I'm better than the Patriots on the football field," she said, nodding vigorously. "So ... what did you think of Mack?" She had to turn the attention away from herself. She was still close to tears, but it was because Mack was so great, not because he'd made her sad. Yet the fear of being destroyed emotionally was there as well.

"He's the best!" Josh yelled.

"Hey." Hyde lifted his hands, palms up. "I thought I was the best."

"Oh! Sorry, Hyde." Josh grinned. "You're the best best, but Mack is definitely the second best."

"Whew. I thought I got replaced for a minute."

Everyone laughed.

"He seems like a really nice guy," Sariah's mom said.

Her dad nodded. "Not sure we can handle any more famous, burly football players in the family though." He inclined his chin to Hyde.

Hyde smiled. "Yeah, I think I need to be the only one."

Sariah rolled her eyes. "You all need to relax. We've been on two dates."

"He tracked you down from Georgia and came to church and the family dinner. I think that's a little more serious than two dates," Lily said.

Caleb rolled his eyes. "I hope I don't have to be that persistent when I find the woman I love."

"It's not love," Sariah protested. The word persistent gave her both hope and fear. Mack said she could reject him 1009 times and he'd keep coming back. Was he just a smooth talker or could he really feel as deeply for her as he seemed to.

"I love him," Josh said. He started running for the house. "Who wants to play catch?"

Sariah wrapped her arms around herself, chilled suddenly and wanting to be inside.

Caleb and Hyde said they'd play. Everyone else started filtering back toward the front door. Hyde stopped and edged in close to Sariah. "Are you feeling comfortable with Mack?"

"He's a really nice guy, Hyde."

"I know. You've just been through so much."

"I'm not made of glass, bro. I'll be fine."

His dark eyes filled with relief. "So, you told him about the fire, and Tyler and ... Denise?"

She shook her head jerkily, her stomach filling with acid. Someday, she'd have to tell Mack. What would happen then? "He knows something's wrong, but he wants me to get to know him, trust him, before I tell him."

Hyde nodded. "That's pretty standup of him."

"He gets my vote for stud of the year."

Josh barreled out of the house with a football tucked under his arm. He slammed into Hyde. "Let's play!"

Hyde picked him up and softly tackled him onto the ground. "I already tackled you."

"No fair," Josh hollered, laughing.

Sariah watched their antics, but her mind had driven away with Mack. How long did she have until he either saw her deformity or found out about it? Maybe it was smarter to tell him soon, but she wanted more carefree time with him. Time before it all crashed down.

CHAPTER FOURTEEN

Sariah shoved her water bottle and her phone in her purse and headed toward the front exit. Jane walked out of one of the treatment rooms.

"Relax yourself into a coma this weekend," Sariah said.

Jane smiled. "Sounds lovely. Have you heard if they've found Scarlett Lily?"

Sariah shook her head. It was the big story this week that Scarlett Lily had disappeared from her Newport Beach home, not taking her cell phone or her Audi. The police weren't leaking any details but the media were in a frenzy about it.

"Don't you know her?"

Jane was Sariah's closest friend at school and Sariah had made the mistake of saying Scarlett was even more beautiful in person when Jane had been dying over pictures of the hockey star, Josh Porter, and Scarlett Lily last fall.

"I only saw her at a party." She prayed nightly for Scarlett's safety. She didn't know her but Sariah had always thought she seemed like a genuine and beautiful person. It was sickening to think of her disappearing and what she might be going through.

"Your life is insane, my friend. Scarlett Lily at parties. Your sister getting ready to marry Hyde Metcalf. And best of all, you're dating Mack Quinn." She squealed. "He's so hot. Only somebody as gorgeous as you could feel worthy to be by Mack Quinn's side."

Sariah smiled but her gut twisted. She and Mack had been texting all week and last weekend he had shown exactly how great he was. She was the farthest thing from gorgeous, or worthy to be by Mack's side. He should have someone like those perfect women at Bucky Buchanan's Super Bowl celebration.

"See ya," Sariah said and hurried away before Jane could say more. She burst out of the front door. It was chilly but not unbearable. She didn't see Mack so she walked toward the parking lot. Several of her classmates walked past and said good-bye. Discreetly looking in windows, she couldn't find Mack sitting in any of the vehicles. Not sure which rental he would have this week, she pulled out her phone to text him as she paced the now nearly-empty parking lot to keep warm. She could climb into her car, but he'd probably be here soon. She hoped. Her deep-seated trust issues reared up and she worried. What if he didn't come? What if he realized she wasn't a perfect model and moved on?

"Hey, lady," a rough voice said from right next to her.

Sariah jumped back and clung to her phone. The man was rough-looking with scraggly hair and a long beard, dirty clothes and face. His blue eyes were cloudy and darted all over her body and then back to her face. He gave her a smile that looked more like a grimace, revealing tobacco-stained teeth. Sariah took a quick breath and said a prayer. She didn't want to hold to stereotypes, but she also didn't want to be alone with this man.

Her eyes darted around. Was Mack coming? Was anyone else around that could help her if this guy proved as dangerous as he looked?

She backed up another step.

"Got any spare change?" he asked.

Sariah clung to her phone and her purse. She didn't have cash of any kind. "I'm sorry, I don't," she said.

"Liar," he spit at her. "Give me some cash." He stepped up closer.

Sariah shook her head. "I don't carry any cash."

"Then give me that purse and I'll see what a liar you are."

He grabbed at her purse.

"No!" Sariah whipped her body away from him so he couldn't grab her purse. He tugged at her hair and she screamed.

Tires rumbled into the parking lot and a door slammed. Sariah looked up to see Mack storming toward them.

"Mack," she sighed. He'd come.

The man released her and turned to face Mack. He squealed and tried to dart away. Mack grabbed his arm and shoved him to the ground. "Stay there," Mack demanded.

Sariah barely had time to reposition her hair around her scars before Mack's blue gaze was sweeping over her. "Are you okay?"

She nodded.

Mack wrapped his arm around her, bringing warmth and reassurance. He pulled out his phone and dialed 911. As soon as he started telling the operator about an attempted assault the man tried to crawl away.

"Don't try it," Mack warned.

The man stared up at him. His eyes were still cloudy but they were filled with terror. Sariah wondered what he saw. As drugged out as he seemed, Mack probably looked like a terrifying giant instead of the gentle, kind man that he was. She cuddled into his side. He glanced down at her and tenderly kissed her forehead, whispering, "Sorry, dinner might be a little late tonight."

She smiled and wrapped both arms around his strong abdomen. "As long as I'm with you I don't care." A truer statement had never come from her lips. Mack was massive and could probably best anyone who threatened her, but he was a gentle giant with her. She'd never felt so safe and desired. Maybe all her fears and trust issues could be resolved with Mack. He'd come for her tonight, exactly when she needed him. Would it be possible that he'd always come for her?

Sirens pierced the air and the man jumped to his feet and tried to make a run for it. Mack released her and flew after him, tackling him to the ground and holding him there until the policemen leapt from their vehicles with their guns drawn.

Mack slowly stood with his hands up, as per their instructions. Sariah's breath whooshed out of her at the beauty of this muscular superman. She wanted to spend every minute getting to know him. When he was with her, she felt as if she didn't need to worry about anything.

CHAPTER FIFTEEN

The next two months passed by in spurts and stops for Mack. Each Saturday afternoon he'd fly to Denver, take Sariah to dinner somewhere different, go to church with her and her family the next day, have dinner with them, and then turn around and fly back. The rest of the week he tried to keep himself busy with training, working with his agent, his sponsors, and his financial people, but Monday through Friday were too slow. All he wanted was more time with Sariah, but as promised he tried to take things slow with her.

He bought a second house in Marietta, only a couple miles from Bucky's mansion. The house was much too large for a single guy but it was in a beautiful wooded area and his tax advisors said he needed a write-off. He couldn't get himself to sleep there and still lived in his downtown Atlanta condo. The house was too far away from the gym and the field were his excuses, but he knew the real reason was he wanted to be in that beautiful house with

Sariah. He'd fallen in love with her. He'd fallen in love with her family. Even Hyde was great to be around now and Josh was his favorite. If only Sariah would trust him with her secret. He was very careful to never touch the right side of her face or neck and her hair always covered it.

Hyde and Lily's wedding was a great day for the family. They'd married on the beach near Hyde's southern California home and been able to keep the paparazzi out for the most part. Mack's agent informed him there were some pictures circulating of him and Sariah from the wedding, but the publicity was good.

Scarlett Lily had returned from what most sources were claiming was an abduction. She declined commenting on her disappearance, no matter how much pressure the media put on her. Jade had sworn up and down that Griff was somehow involved but Griff wouldn't admit anything to Mack when he tried to call him, telling him he was on an undercover job in Panama and couldn't talk.

Mid-May on a Monday night, Mack was feeling the letdown of another five days before he saw Sariah again. His busy season was starting up soon. In June they'd be back to mandatory practices. Something had to change with him and Sariah. Soon he'd be too busy to fly to her. They'd been texting back and forth tonight and a few seconds ago she'd casually mentioned something about having vacation time from school. Mack pushed dial immediately after seeing the text.

"Just needed to hear my voice?" Sariah asked.

"Always." He stood and paced his apartment, ideas forming in his mind. "You have vacation time?"

She hesitated then said, "Yes."

"Would you go away with me somewhere?"

"Where?" Her voice squeaked. Why was she so nervous?

"Anywhere you want." It hit him why she might be concerned. They'd kissed, but never anything more than that. "We'd get separate rooms."

"I know, it's not that."

"What is it?"

No response.

His grip on the phone tightened. "Please, Sariah. I just want uninterrupted time with you. These past two months I've loved being with you, getting to know you and your family, but I ... I really want more time than these short weekend trips. Just a few days. Please."

"Okay," she squeaked out.

"Yes!" he hollered.

"Calm down, you didn't win the Super Bowl again."

"It feels like it. Thank you." He sank into his leather sofa. "Where do you want to go? We could fly anywhere. Is there a spot you've dreamed of seeing?" He didn't care where, just as long as they were together. He usually flew commercial but he could charter a jet, or have Kaleb send his jet, or have Griff come fly them in a helicopter, if he wasn't on some clandestine mission. Where to, though? He would love to get Sariah somewhere warm. Their trip to California with her family for the wedding was only for the day and they hadn't had time to swim in the ocean. Kissing on the beach sounded too good to be true. But wait. She might not want to be in a swimsuit. Whatever she was hiding on her neck, she hid it well. He'd never seen her in anything that didn't have a decent collar and long sleeves, even on warm days.

"Why don't we drive to Crested Butte for a few days?" she suggested.

"Crested what?"

She laughed. "Crested Butte. It's about fours away. It's beautiful there. We could go on hikes and mountain bike rides and just chill and relax together."

It wasn't a tropical island but he really didn't care. He'd get to be with Sariah. "When could you go?"

"Let's go to church with my family on Sunday and then we can leave after dinner. I'll get Tuesday and Wednesday off school."

"I'll get hotel rooms booked. Thank you."

"Happy to serve," she quipped.

He smiled.

"Truly, I'm like a puppy waiting to chew on your shoe. I can hardly wait."

Mack chuckled at another one of her cute analogies. "Neither can I."

They talked for a few more minutes then said goodnight. Mack thought this might be the weekend. Maybe she'd finally trust him enough to show him her neck, tell him about whatever happened, and maybe he'd finally get brave enough to tell her he loved her.

He was clutching his phone and jumped when it buzzed with an incoming text. He clicked on the text from Griff, but the phone kept buzzing. Griff must be sending a bunch of texts. It opened up to a picture. Mack squinted at it. He couldn't see the woman's face but wet, dark hair trailed along a neck and shoulder that were badly scarred. Maybe burns? Had Griff made a mistake and sent him something from an op that was meant for Sutton Smith, or one of his buddies?

He scrolled through as if watching a horror show. The pictures showed a misshapen ear and more angles of the burned neck, shoulder, and upper arm. It looked like someone was holding the person in place and had ripped their shirt off, as only the strap of a bra was visible. The seventh or eighth picture down showed the person's face. The breath rushed out of him and Mack collapsed onto his sofa.

"Sariah," he murmured.

It was her beautiful face, full of anguish. A hand grasped her chin and though Sariah looked furious with her dark eyes full of fire, she also looked beaten and disgraced.

The next text down was a book from the normally brief Griff, "Thought you should see these. The story is they almost drowned her before taking these pictures of her and putting the pictures all over the internet with a story about Tyler Whittingham burning her every time she cheated on him."

Mack sat there, staring at the pictures. Someone had almost

drowned Sariah? Someone else had burned her for cheating on him? That part had to be lies. The Sariah he knew was without guile, she'd never cheat on anyone. But if she'd had a boyfriend who had abused her like that ... Mack's fists clenched as venomous thoughts he'd never had before circled in his mind.

He wished he hadn't seen this. It had been over two months, no, since he'd first seen her last fall almost eight months ago, that he'd been falling in love with Sariah, and hoping she'd tell him about what had happened to her. He didn't want to find out like this, with partial facts and a sick gut. Why would Griff do this to him? He clenched his fist. This wasn't Griff's fault. Griff didn't relate to things like emotion and love, but he protected and took care of his family. In his mind, he was protecting Mack by making sure he had all the facts.

He couldn't respond though. He wanted to ask so many questions and that wasn't fair to Sariah. When she was ready she would tell him the answers. He rolled his neck, wondering when she would ever trust him enough to confide in him. Only two more weeks and he'd be too busy to see her much, especially if she wasn't willing to relocate to Georgia when she graduated from school in June. Would their relationship fizzle and die? His chest tightened at the thought.

He had this weekend. A weekend with only him and Sariah. His chance to really grow close to her, and pray she'd share her secrets. He didn't want to force her into sharing. Yet how could he act like he didn't know now that he knew and would that be worse for their relationship when she found out?

His phone rang. He glanced at it, not wanting to talk to anybody but Sariah and with no clue what he'd say to her. Navy.

He slid it open. "Hey, sis."

"You okay?" Her usually flippant voice was full of concern.

"Griff told you?"

"I'm sorry. He just got back from two months undercover in Panama. I chatted with him a little bit about you and Sariah. I didn't know he'd go and find those pictures. He said they were online. Big blow-up about four years ago with some guy who was hoping to get into politics and his girlfriend did that to Sariah while they were dating."

"Stop. I don't want to hear this from you. I want her to tell me."

"How long have you been going to see her every weekend?"

"A couple of months."

Navy said nothing, which was worse than her telling him how gullible he was. The pictures and disturbing story were making him sick and he knew it was reasonable of his family to think Sariah should have told him her secrets by now, but they didn't know her like he did. Sariah was feisty, funny, beautiful, and smart, but she was also very private and guarded. If he forced his way past her barriers, it might be the end of their relationship. He couldn't let that happen, but now that he had some of the information, how could he just act as if everything was normal?

CHAPTER SIXTEEN

Sariah and Mack arrived in Crested Butte late Sunday. It was too late for her to play tour guide and reveal how gorgeous this mountain retreat was. They had three days together. She could show him the wonders of the mountains and share all her secrets as well. She'd promised herself that this would be the weekend. She'd finally tell him about her scars, what had happened with Tyler, and how much she loved Mack.

Last night, when he arrived to take her to dinner, and today things had been a little... uncomfortable was the only word she could think of, between them. She wasn't sure what to pin it on. Her nervousness for him to see her scars and hear her story? It could be possible something was off with Mack. He'd seemed really excited when she agreed Monday night to go away together, but maybe he was nervous also. Maybe he had his own secrets he was nervous to share. She smiled to herself, knowing that probably wasn't true. Mack was an open book.

They loaded up into the elevator after checking into The Grand Lodge. It was very nice but not over-the-top extravagant. She liked that. Mack was always real and down-to-earth. She knew he had plenty of money and was famous in his own right, but he never acted like that. Even when people recognized him and asked for autographs, he'd simply give them his irresistible grin, sign whatever they wanted, and then turn the conversation around and get to know them a little bit. He never bragged about himself.

They exited the elevator and walked to their suite. Sariah opened the door, as Mack had insisted he carry the luggage. Nerves fluttered in her stomach as they walked in. He'd promised separate bedrooms, and she trusted Mack implicitly, but they'd never been alone like this. The main part of the suite had a nice-sized living room with a kitchenette. She could see two bedrooms, with lamps softly lighting them.

Mack carried her luggage to one and his to the other. He returned to where she stood by the front door.

Smiling, he took the key from her hand and set it on a side table. Then he slid her purse off her shoulder and also set it down. He wrapped both of his hands around hers and asked, "Are you tired?"

She nodded, her throat feeling thick. This was going to be the time to reveal all and she was terrified. She should probably wait until the last night they were together. Then if he wanted some space it wouldn't be as awkward. That was good reasoning.

He tugged her toward the bedroom where he'd put her suitcase. "You should rest then. I've got a lot planned for tomorrow."

"Do you now?" She forced a smile and berated herself for feeling awkward. This was Mack. He was amazing. She could probably rip down her shirt and push her hair out of the way and he'd tell her how beautiful she was and hold her while she told him the whole awful story. Probably.

She looked up into his blue gaze as he stopped in the doorframe of her room. Not tonight though.

"But I do need at least one good night kiss to get me through until morning."

She laughed, sliding her arms around his neck. "Do you now?" she asked again.

He grinned and his hands encompassed her lower back. His lips met hers and joy encircled her as he gave her a passionate kiss that displaced all worries from her mind. They'd kissed every Saturday night and Sunday afternoon for the past couple of months, standing next to one of their cars. Something about being alone, in this lovely room, took the intimacy of this kiss to a deeper level.

Mack pulled her up and in, ever closer to his strong body, and then he deepened the kiss. Her mouth seemed to explode with tingles and warmth. Mack tilted his head and continued the exploration of her mouth. His kiss became more insistent and filled with passion. He picked her clean off the floor and pressed her against the door as he continued working his magic on her mouth.

Sariah had never, ever felt a kiss as deeply as she did this one. She loved it, but there were warning bells going off in the back of her mind. Ignoring them, she wrapped her legs around Mack's back and clung to his broad shoulders with her hands.

Mack pushed off the door, and still kissing her, he walked slowly into the bedroom. The warning bells became fire sirens. Sariah's body was on fire and she needed a pump truck to knock her over with water, right now. She pulled away from Mack's kiss, gulped in air, and said loudly, "Please help us, dear Father in Heaven, to stop being stupid."

Mack stopped in his tracks and stared at her, his breath coming hard and fast. He set her on her feet, stepped back and said, "You are an angel, Sariah."

She backed away, bumping into the bed. "No, I'm not. I just kissed you like ..." She couldn't even say it. She'd heard Pastor warn about it, but had no clue passion could explode that quickly. She felt like she'd been consumed by fire and desire. Her prayer had been spot on. It was very, very stupid to risk their virtue and the purity of their developing relationship like that.

Mack's blue gaze was very serious. "That was on me." He shoved a hand through his short curls. "I love you, Sariah, and I let myself get carried away. It won't happen again."

Sariah believed him, and trusted him, but she had to go back to the first part of his statement. "You love me?"

He nodded and then shook his head. "I'm messing this all up. I wanted to tell you how I loved you in a beautiful way. Not when ... I'd almost taken advantage of you."

Sariah smiled softly at him. "You are a great man, Mack Quinn. We both let things get a little ... heated, but I don't believe you would ever take advantage of me." She stepped up to him, stood on tiptoes and softly kissed him. "And I love you too."

Mack's chest rose and fell quickly. "I want to keep kissing you so badly right now."

"But you love me too much to start that fire again," she guessed.

He blinked down at her and tenderly cupped the left side of her face with his right hand. "Exactly." He backed away, his hand dropping to his side. "Tomorrow I'll give you the kiss I'm dying to give you right now."

She tilted her head and tried for sass, but her heart was beating so fast she could hardly speak. "I'll plan on that, Mr. Quinn."

He grinned and then turned and hurried from the room, closing the door behind him. She heard his door shut as well. Sariah stood there until her heart stopping racing. That kiss had been insane and far too much for her inexperienced self to deal with. Tyler had tried to push her physically a few times, but she'd never felt desire like this and it had been easy to tell him no. Keeping her desires in control with Mack was definitely going to be a challenge, but Mack was a good man ... a great man.

Her face heated up as she remembered how she'd said a prayer aloud. Some people would make fun of her for that. Not Mack. He'd told her she was an angel. She put a hand to her heart. She loved him so much. Maybe telling him her secrets wouldn't be anything horrific like she'd envisioned.

CHAPTER SEVENTEEN

Mack followed Sariah on his rented mountain bike along the Snodgrass Trail above Crested Butte. Everything in this valley was so lush and green. He was used to green, being from Rhode Island and living in Georgia, but the mountains and pine trees in Colorado were majestic and he loved the crisp, clean air.

Sariah kept up a good pace. He liked letting her lead. He was still humiliated thinking about last night. He'd almost let the fire for Sariah race out of control. He'd never had that happen to him before. He was almost afraid for tonight, but he'd be more careful. He loved that she'd stopped and said a vocal prayer. She was everything he'd always wanted. Now if only she'd tell him about her scars, and those horrible pictures. Did he bring it up or just keep waiting? He'd told her he loved her and she'd responded. He was still waiting for the perfect moment this morning to give her the kiss he'd promised last night. It had better be in a public place.

They finished the trail and returned the bikes to the concierge who had secured them from a local bike shop and ate a quick lunch in the hotel restaurant. Then they drove to the Judd Falls Trail, a trail that was supposed to be fabulous and was close to their hotel.

Again, Sariah set a great pace and they enjoyed looking down at Judd Falls then set off on the higher trail to the lake that was another four miles, if the people they'd questioned on the trail had accurate info. Mack's gaze kept being pulled from the forest and towering mountain peaks to Sariah.

He was busy studying her beautiful frame and when she stopped suddenly, he almost plowed her over.

"You okay?" he asked, resting his hands on her waist.

"M-m-mack," she whispered, turning toward him and clinging to his arm.

Hearing the fear in her voice, Mack stepped in front of her and searched for the source. A large black bear was down in the stream below the trail. The animal was busy searching for fish and hadn't noticed them.

Mack wasn't sure how to proceed. Black bears weren't as dangerous as grizzlies but he knew they'd killed humans, Mack and Sariah were on his territory, and he hadn't seen any other hikers for a while.

Mack reached back for Sariah. "Let's just head slowly back," he whispered.

She didn't respond but started walking back down the trail.

Mack kept looking over his shoulder, his eyes on the bear as they eased quietly down the trail. Voices drifted down to him from farther up the trail. Mack's gaze darted back to the bear. The bear's head swiveled to the voices and it stopped searching for fish and watched to see who was approaching through the trees. Mack's stomach dropped when he saw two teenage girls jogging down the trail, talking rapidly, not a care in the world. They were both small and that worried Mack. A bear might be threatened by someone his size, but not a skinny near-child.

The bear must've had the same thought as it lumbered up the short incline straight toward the girls.

"Sariah," Mack muttered, ripping his keys out and putting them in her hand. "Run down to the Jeep. If I don't come with the girls soon, get help."

"I can't leave you," she whispered back.

"Go!" He pushed at her and started back up the trail.

The bear reached the trail and planted itself in the girls' path. They both stopped abruptly, twenty feet from the bear, and their mouths dropped open in horror. The bear lifted up onto two feet and the girls screamed in unison. The bear roared in response. Mack's stomach churned, but he had no choice. He yelled as loud as he could, a deep, guttural yell that didn't sound human, even to him.

The bear pivoted to face him, obviously recognizing the real threat. Mack prayed for help as he stomped toward the bear, screaming, "Go!" He'd never felt small around another human, but this bear on his hind paws had him by almost a foot. His stomach filled with ice but he kept moving, and praying he looked bigger than he felt.

C old sweat covered her body as Sariah watched Mack storm up the trail toward the bear. The bravery in that man astounded her, but the fear of the bear ripping him apart had her shoving the keys in her pocket and instead of running, like he'd told her to, she searched for sharp rocks and sticks. She'd been raised in the Colorado mountains by a forest ranger. She knew the textbook answers on how to fight black bears, but she'd always been afraid to run into one. Mack's intention was obviously to protect the girls, but she was afraid he was going to enrage the bear with his aggressive yell and movements. Yet if he didn't distract the bear, the animal would probably rip into one of those girls.

The girls were still screaming and the bear reared up and roared. He obviously felt threatened, and from the way he went after the girls initially he must think they were easy prey. If there was any hope of this bear leaving without a fight, they'd just lost it.

Mack was big and loud and he looked like a superhero as he kept fearlessly approaching the bear. The girls had scuttled back on the trail, away from the bear. They were hugging each other and still screaming.

"Go!" Mack hollered at the bear, shooing him with his hands like he was a pesky dog.

Sariah was amazed at his bravery, but the bear stood his ground.

With black bears you were supposed to fight, not run or play dead. Mack definitely looked ready for a fight but a man's flesh couldn't withstand the claws or teeth of a bear. Sariah scooped up another large rock and then she spotted a good, solid stick.

The bear growled back, slammed onto his front paws, and advanced on Mack on all fours. He was a massive animal, making even Mack look small.

The girls screeched out their terror. They couldn't have been more than fifteen or sixteen. Sariah didn't blame them for being scared, but she wished they'd stop screaming and adding to the commotion.

Mack raised his muscular arms and roared right back. The bear kept coming. Mack didn't back down. He bravely took two more steps forward.

"Hey!" Sariah yelled. She dodged around Mack's side, wound up and threw the larger of the rocks she'd been holding. It pinged off the bear's side. The bear yelped and stopped advancing.

"Sariah," Mack cried out, pushing her behind him. "Stay back."

Sariah shoved the stick she'd found into his hand. "If he keeps coming, hit him with that." She bent and picked up another rock, stepping to Mack's side and hurling it as hard as she could at the bear. It hit him in the head and he roared in anger. "Let's back up toward the mountain so it will know it can retreat to the river." It had come from the river, so hopefully that was where it wanted to retreat, if it wanted to retreat.

Mack nodded and holding the stick high above his head, he waited until Sariah was behind him then he slowly retreated a few steps with her. The bear turned slightly with them, staying focused on Mack and not retreating like Sariah had hoped. At least the girls were just whimpering now, and had followed their example and moved farther away from the bear and its path to the river.

Sariah waited, holding her breath. She glanced askance at Mack. He looked like a fearless warrior, holding the stick in a threatening position, the muscles in his arms all flexed and ready for action. She loved him. This man could protect her from anything. If they survived this, she was going to kiss him and tell him her every secret.

The bear shuffled forward, snarling at them.

"Throw stuff at him," Sariah said. She bent and scooped rocks, flinging them as fast and hard as she could at the bear. Mack followed her advice and her eyes widened as she saw he picked up huge rocks and launched them so hard at the bear, the bear was knocked backward. The bear didn't advance on them but it didn't scurry away either. Sariah was breathing hard as she kept scooping and launching but she was running out of decent-sized rocks and so was Mack. He'd dropped the stick she'd given him to throw rocks. He picked it up, aimed it like a javelin and threw it hard. It was too blunt to penetrate, but it knocked the bear backward.

The bear sort of whined then pivoted and lumbered back down to the stream. Within seconds it had crossed the stream and was hidden by the trees on the other side. Sariah's breath rushed out of her and she deflated.

Mack's arms came around her. He squeezed her close. "You were amazing," he said.

Sariah stared up at him. "It was all you. Schnikies! You can throw hard for a lineman. Maybe we should push the Rocket out of his position."

He smiled and kissed her firmly. "I love you. How did you know exactly what to do? I thought I was supposed to posture, but that didn't scare it."

"My dad taught me. With black bears who've gone after people, many people have been able to fight them off."

He kissed her again. "You're my hero."

Sariah laughed. "Back at you."

"Thank you," the girls were next to them and they kept repeating thank you over and over again.

Sariah hadn't even noticed them approach.

"Can we walk down with you?" the redheaded girl asked.

Mack nodded. "Sure. Let's get you two out of here."

"I can't believe you just fought that bear." The blonde girl stared up at Mack with wide eyes. "You're so hot. Way hotter and tougher than ..." She shook her head as if grasping for a heroic enough figure in her mind. "Than Thor!"

Her redhead friend nodded her agreement. "Thank you," she said much more quietly than her friend.

Sariah bit at her lip to keep from laughing. Mack's face darkened with embarrassment.

"We'd better go," he muttered. He gestured in front of him and the girls scurried down the trail, obviously still shaken from the encounter with the bear. The blonde girl kept looking back at Mack with longing and worship in her eyes.

Mack and Sariah walked together behind them. He checked over his shoulder and she followed his gaze, but the bear was thankfully gone. Mack put his arm around her. "You okay?" he asked.

"Of course, always okay with the hero who's hotter and stronger than Thor with me." She batted her eyelashes at him.

He squeezed her arm and laughed. "Don't share that one with anyone."

She smiled. "Ammunition is always good to have."

He bent and swiftly kissed her. "I still say you're the hero today."

Sariah pointed ahead of her. "They don't seem to think so."

The girls both glanced back at them and the blonde winked boldly at Mack. When they turned around, Mack rolled his eyes. Sariah laughed but she kept her arm around his waist and stayed close to him. He was the hero and luckily for her, he loved her.

CHAPTER EIGHTEEN

After the craziness of fighting the bear, they hiked back to Mack's rented Durango, said goodbye to his teenage girl fans, and drove to the hotel. They showered, ate a nice dinner in downtown Crested Butte at Marchitelli's Gourmet Noodle, and then went back to the hotel. Sariah knew she had to show Mack tonight. She had an idea of how to do it. She hoped he would understand the level of trust she was putting in him.

They walked into their room hand in hand and she turned to him. "Do you want to go sit in the hot tub?"

Mack's eyes filled with questions, but he nodded. "If you want to."

"I do." She squeezed his hand and hurried to her room. Slowly sliding into the swimming suit she'd bought in preparation for this trip, a thrill of fear darted through her. She'd never worn a swimming suit without a long-sleeved rash guard over it. This was braver than facing down a bear. She pulled her hair up into a ponytail. Her neck felt naked, exposed.

Taking a deep breath, she side-stepped very slowly to the vanity mirror. Her left side appeared first and she thought she looked fit and pretty good in the floral swimsuit. Gradually she eased over until her middle and then her right side appeared. She froze. The sight of her bumpy, disgusting skin made her stomach drop. The fire had disfigured her ear, neck, right shoulder, and part of her upper arm.

Seeing the scars revealed fully in her one-piece swimsuit robbed her of the bravery she'd felt as she put it on. She couldn't go out there and face Mack. Would he recoil from her or would his eyes simply fill with pity? Mack was such a good man, but how could a man that was perfect like him want someone disfigured like her? She couldn't do this. Didn't want to know the answers to those questions.

Pacing the small room, she realized she had to either put a shirt on and take her hair down to go to the hot tub or change her clothes and tell him she didn't feel like hot tubbing now. She knew Mack would take either option in stride, but why couldn't she trust him to take her scars in stride?

As she passed the mirror, she caught another glimpse of the disfigured skin. For some reason she pictured Scarlett Lily in her black dress at that Super Bowl party months ago. Scarlett's skin was so smooth and beautiful and Mack had said she knew his brother. The Quinn family were all perfectly beautiful. How dare Sariah think she could fit in their world? Her stomach flipped again. What should she do? She simply couldn't face him like this. Mack was so amazing and she didn't want to lose him.

She dropped to the floor next to the bed. Kneeling, she bowed her head and begged for help. A calm reassurance flooded her and the remembrance, *Jesus loves you.*

She knew it was true. Jesus did love her and he would give her strength. Struggling to her feet, she knew at some point she had to focus on the fact that she was enough in God's eyes. She trusted Jesus. She had to trust that if Mack was the man for her, he would love her regardless.

She picked up the coverup she'd brought to wear down to the hot tub, put a hand on her stomach to quell the nervousness, walked slowly to the door of her room, and yanked it open. This was it. Mack's reaction would determine where they went from here. She'd never loved a man like she did him and she muttered a prayer that he wouldn't recoil or run from her. He'd faced down a bear. Doubtful he was going to run from some scars. These encouraging thoughts had her walking out of her room and into the main area. She reached up to pull her hair in front of her neck before remembering it was secured in a ponytail. Forcing herself to drop her hand to her side she wrung the coverup in her hand and squeezed her eyes shut, terrified of his reaction.

She heard his soft melodious voice, "Sariah."

Focusing on Mack's face, she braced herself for his reaction. His eyes traveled slowly over her right side but didn't linger there for long. His eyes continued down, taking in the floral suit and her legs then coming back up to rest on her face. He smiled at her. "You look ... so beautiful."

Sariah's breath caught. He'd seen her scars but hadn't really focused on them. She could see that he wasn't blowing any smoke, but truly thought she was beautiful. Sariah dropped the coverup on the floor and ran at him. Mack opened his arms and she hugged him tight, fully appreciating the finely-honed muscles of his chest and abdomen pressed against her.

Staring up into his handsome face she finally mustered up the courage to ask, "You don't care about ... the scars?"

Mack shook his head. He tenderly bent and kissed the mottled skin on the right side of her neck. Sariah thought she would feel disgusted and embarrassed if anyone ever touched her scars, but Mack's acceptance made warmth dart through her. He ran his fingers along her shoulder and neck and she quivered from his touch. She didn't have much feeling there but knowing that he was touching her scars so calmly made her love him even more.

Pulling back, he smiled. "I'd better stop or I'll have more trouble staying in control than I did last night."

Sariah could hardly believe how perfect he was. "You're actually ... attracted to me right now?"

A loud breath popped out of him. "Oh, Sariah. If you could only see how incredible you look right now." He smiled. "I promised you I wouldn't kiss you too much again, but you in this swimsuit, looking so beautiful." He shook his head. "We'd better get to a public place quick."

He took her hand and started toward the door. Sariah tugged at him. "You aren't grossed out by my scars, or embarrassed of them?"

He shook his head. "I think scars add character. Wait until you see my brother, Griff. His entire back was burned by a bomb. He saved my sister-in-law, Jasmine's life that night." He touched her neck again and Sariah trembled from the tenderness of it. "How were you burned?" His brow furrowed, as if he was concerned what her answer would be.

She stared at him, dumbfounded by his acceptance. Months she'd been afraid and waiting to show him her disfigurement, and he took it in stride as if she'd just told him about a childhood skiing accident where she hurt her knee or something. "Campfire," she muttered. "I was five."

Relief flashed across his face, which confused her. Where did he think she'd gotten the scars? "That must've been terrifying for your parents."

"Yeah. My mom still won't talk about it. I think she likes me covering it up." She paused and then asked, "Do you like me covering it up?"

He shook his head. "Every part of you is beautiful to me. If you're more comfortable with your hair over your neck that's fine, but I don't think you should cover it up. It's part of you. You're beautiful."

Wow. Sariah was still trying to process his awesomeness. Blushing, she walked over and picked up the white coverup and slid it over her head. Mack walked slowly to her. His gaze was intense and the most beautiful smoldering look she'd ever seen.

He fingered the sleeve of her coverup. "You can wear this if you want," he said in a deep, throaty voice, "But don't wear it for me."

Sariah felt warm all over. Who needed a hot tub? "You don't care if I strut down to the hot tub without anything over my suit?"

He shook his head. "I think you should share your beauty with everyone."

Sariah searched his gaze and the sincerity, desire, and love there had her body pulsing with joy and acceptance. "I won't wear it then," she whispered.

Mack's gaze heated her even more. He reached down and grasped the edges of the coverup. His fingers brushed against her thighs. He pulled it up her body in one of the most tender and tantalizing moves she'd ever experienced. Lifting it over her head, he dropped it to the floor and then his eyes slowly traveled over her again.

"So beautiful," he whispered.

Sariah stared up into his blue eyes. "Have I told you how much I love you?" she asked.

Mack smiled. He bent low and kissed her. "I love you," he murmured, then he kissed her again. The kisses quickly grew in intensity and Sariah didn't even flinch when his palms framed her face and his fingers grazed her scars.

Mack drew back first. "Like I said, we'd better get to a public place quick."

"Don't want a repeat of last night?" she teased, feeling light and happy and so in love. Soon she'd tell him about the other nightmare associated with her scars, but she didn't want to tarnish this moment, or how she felt with Mack looking at her with such devotion and desire.

"No, ma'am. Especially not with you in a swimming suit. Whoo."
He blew out a breath. "And those girls today claimed *I* was hot."

She laughed and let him escort her out of the suite and toward
the elevator. Mack thought she was hot, even with her scars. She
had officially found the perfect man for her. She loved him
so much.

CHAPTER NINETEEN

Mack woke up at six the next morning, feeling like he could conquer the world. His legs actually were a little stiff from the biking and hiking but he needed a really intense weight workout today. He left a note for Sariah and texted her phone but she didn't respond, she must be still asleep, then he headed for the hotel gym. It was decent, as far as hotel gyms went. He worked out for a couple of hours before hurrying back to their suite. He couldn't wait to be with Sariah again. Today they were going to bike on the trails around town, buy some bear spray, do a hike to Meridian, or Long Lake, as the locals called it, and maybe paddleboard the river. It wasn't warm enough to want to get wet, but Sariah had proven how brave she was.

He smiled as he swung the suite door open and rushed for his bedroom. Sariah's door was still closed, but it was only eight-thirty. He hurried to get into the shower. Even though they would get sweaty again hiking, he didn't want to stink like a gym rat. Last night they'd gone to their separate rooms after hot tubbing. He wanted to be careful not to put them in a compromising situation, but this time with Sariah was just about perfect. There was only one worry. He still hadn't told her that Griff had sent him those pictures and he'd already known about her scars. Would she be upset? His stomach churned at the thought. He didn't want to keep anything from her, but last night she'd needed his love and acceptance, not more questions about how the scars had caused her torture and trauma.

As he got out of the shower, he heard Sariah's door open and close. Then he heard his bedroom door open. He hurried to slide into his pants and opened his bathroom door, steam following him out. Sariah was waiting just inside the bedroom door. He noticed her hair was covering her right side again. Had they regressed from last night? Had he not responded correctly, shown her exactly how beautiful she was to him?

"Hey." He smiled but she didn't return it. "What's wrong?" Mack hurried across the small bedroom to her.

She held aloft her phone. Anger flashed in her eyes, but she also looked very vulnerable and beautiful right now. "This is wrong, Mack. I knew I shouldn't fall for somebody famous."

"What's going on?"

She shoved the phone against his chest. Mack took it and scrolled through the article, some online celebrity magazine. "Has another impoverished Udy girl captured a famous Patriots' player's heart?" was the first line. He scanned the article. It made Sariah and Lily look like gold diggers who had pulled the wool over Mack and Hyde's eyes. He remembered hearing about stuff like this last spring when Hyde and Lily started dating.

"It's just some stupid ragtag," Mack said. "You can't let stuff like this bug you."

"Oh, I can't? Maybe it would bug *you* if you were the one being made out to be a whore."

"What?"

"Did you not see the pictures?"

Mack shook his head.

"Scroll down."

He obeyed and the pictures started popping up. Somebody had been following them the past couple of days. Crested Butte was a great vacation spot, there were probably other famous people here and these scummy paparazzi had followed them and found Mack and Sariah. Mack didn't think he was notorious enough to have someone tailing him, but his family was. Had he brought this on Sariah? His stomach filled with dread.

There were pictures of them at dinner, walking hand in hand along the quaint main street of town, and several pictures of them walking into their room, one with Sariah tugging on his arm, grinning up at him, with a caption, "Sariah Udy obviously can't wait to sleep her way out of poverty." Then there were the pics of them in the hot tub. Mack's arm was around her shoulder, but her neck and right ear were clearly visible. Below the picture was a caption, "Maybe Mack Quinn doesn't mind a deformed girlfriend, as long as she puts out." He winced. Why were these magazines so harsh and crude? Probably to bring attention and sell ads.

He handed the phone back to Sariah. "I'm sorry that happened. I'll have my agent contact the magazine and take the article down. It's obvious slander."

She glowered at him. "It's all over the internet, Mack. Are you going to fight them all for me? Are you going to protect me from other pictures being taken?"

"Of course, I will." He caught her hand. "Sariah, I'm serious about how much I love you. These lying articles don't matter to me."

"Well, they matter to me." She pulled her hand back. "And I want the truth from you right now."

"Okay." What truth?

"I couldn't get over it last night, how great you reacted to seeing my deformity. How kind you were. Then it hit me."

His stomach sank as she stared pointedly at him, crossing her arms over her chest. "You already knew."

He clenched his fists. Dang Griff and Navy. The only option now was through. "I was going to tell you, but I wanted you to trust me, to share with me."

"You know how important trust is to me." She seemed to shrivel before him as she tucked her hair around her neck. She backed up a step. "And I definitely don't trust you now."

"Sariah, please." He held up a hand. "I didn't go looking for it. My brother sent me some pictures."

Her eyes widened. "*The* pictures?" her voice squeaked.

He nodded. "The ones where somebody is holding you."

Her face blanched and she backed up again.

"Please, Sariah," he said again. There were so many arguments and explanations he wanted to make, but she had to trust him, she just did.

"How long ago did you see them?"

"A week," he admitted.

Her eyes were full of accusations. "And you didn't say anything to me?"

"What did you want me to say?" He tried to not be frustrated, but he was scared this wouldn't end well and he didn't know how to make it better. All he knew was he couldn't lose her. He'd tried his very best to get her to trust him and now he'd muddled it up. "From the first day at your school I knew something was wrong, how could I not? I've been waiting the past couple of months for you to trust me and show me. I didn't want to just force it out of you."

She shook her head, obviously not listening. "You should've told me you saw those pictures. And now this." She held up her phone. "I thought I could trust you."

"Trust goes both ways, Sariah," he tried to say it gently but he needed to say it. "You've never trusted me with your secrets, so how could I gain your trust without you granting it?"

"I tried to grant it last night," she yelled at him. "And now I've been exposed again. I thought you loved me, but you're just going to hurt me like Tyler and Denise did." Whirling from him, she ran through the hotel room, grabbed her purse, and slammed out the door.

Mack followed her. She rushed for the staircase and banged through that door, racing down the stairs.

"Sariah, wait." He didn't have a shirt or socks or shoes on and he didn't have a wallet, but he had to catch her. The grips on the stairs dug into his feet but he ignored it and pumped down the stairs after her.

Sariah was still ahead of him when she burst out at the main level and then ran through the hallway to the main lobby. He'd almost caught her when a little boy darted in front of him in the main lobby. Mack dodged to the side and lost precious seconds avoiding the child. Sariah flew out the front entrance and onto the sidewalk. A man on a motorcycle pulled up and Sariah climbed on the back of his motorcycle.

"Go!" she yelled.

The man looked back at her in surprise.

Mack was almost upon them. "Wait," he hollered.

The man glanced his way and the surprise turned to fear.

"Go!" Sariah pounded at the guy's back.

The guy obeyed, gunning the motorcycle out of the circle drive. Mack ran after them but he had no hope of keeping up as the motorcycle raced down the road. Sariah glanced back at him once. The sadness on her face made him keep running, but they disappeared from sight and he finally accepted defeat. Pebbles were imbedded in his feet. He turned and hobbled quickly back toward the hotel. He prayed the man on that motorcycle would treat her with respect and that Sariah would come back to him. Somehow, someway he was going to find her, and explain better than he just had.

CHAPTER TWENTY

The motorcycle guy was surprisingly nice. He wanted to report Mack as an abusive boyfriend and Sariah had to explain they'd had a disagreement, that Mack was not abusive. He'd hurt her, but she knew he hadn't intended to. Everything hurt though and all she wanted was distance from the pain, the humiliation, and Mack. He'd known, he'd seen those horrific pictures Denise had taken and shared everywhere she could. She tried to force it all from her mind, but couldn't.

The motorcycle guy took her to the Greyhound in Gunnison, and luckily, the bus was only twelve minutes out. As she finally boarded it and rode toward Denver, she wilted into the upholstered seat. It smelled like moldy bread. At least Mack hadn't found her. She felt bad for leaving him and being so dramatic about it, but she needed some distance from the pain right now and sadly he was entwined in that. She couldn't believe how her dating Mack had exploded online. They'd been dating for months, why now? How did someone get a picture of her face and neck in the hot tub, the first time she pulled her hair back in who knew how long? There were so many questions firing in her head. She loved Mack and would expect that his family were good and honorable like him, but would his sister or brother have tipped off the media? How else would they find them and exploit them with the most horrific timing? She hated thinking ill of Mack's family, but she couldn't find another explanation. Unless Denise was coming after her again.

She pulled out her phone and typed in her name, Tyler's name, and Denise's name. The images of Sariah after Denise and her brothers tried to drown her were still there and all the sickening memories returned with them.

Tyler was four years older than her and she'd thought he was so mature, charming, and handsome. She had no idea he had a serious girlfriend in Boulder and had been two-timing both of them the summer after Sariah graduated high school. When Denise found out about Sariah, she'd attacked Tyler and his political aspirations, through attacking Sariah. She'd had her brothers almost drown Sariah in the lake by her house then rip her shirt off. When they discovered her scars, they'd laughed and taken all kinds of pictures of her. The pictures had been posted everywhere on the internet, with Denise claiming Tyler had burned Sariah every time she cheated on him. Sariah hadn't even known about the other girl until she was attacked coming home from work late one night. Denise had served time for it, but Tyler had gotten through the lies, gone on his merry way to becoming a lawyer and was working into politics. Sariah hadn't heard from him in almost four years. Sariah had been the one who'd had to carry the shame of it all. Over the years it seemed people had forgotten, but apparently it was still out there.

How could Mack have seen those pictures and pretended he didn't know? Sariah hated that part of her life. She hated her scars. She hated feeling deformed. She really hated how dirty and disgraceful Denise's attack and Tyler's desertion had left her.

She stared out the window at the mountains and trees. Her phone kept buzzing in her pocket. She finally pulled it out and read the numerous texts from Mack—apologizing, begging her to talk to him, wanting to make sure she was safe. Leaning her head against the seat, tears squeezed down her face. Yesterday had been one of the best days of her life, because of Mack, and now she was second-guessing seeing him again. She finally texted back that she was safe, riding the bus home, and she just needed some space for a little while. It was the best she could do right now.

She should've texted Aunt Allie to pick her up from the bus station but she figured she'd get an Uber. She really didn't want to talk to anybody right now.

She watched the mountains slide by on I-70, alternating between cussing herself for treating Mack so horribly and questioning Mack and his family and everything she believed about their relationship and the trust she'd placed in him. Yet had she really? *Trust goes both ways.* Why hadn't she trusted him with her secret sooner? It probably had just been a matter of time before he found out from someone. There were pictures of her and Mack from Lily and Hyde's wedding. It was inevitable someone would show him the pictures of her scars. At least he hadn't gone looking for them. Maybe if she would've trusted him sooner, they could be dealing with the negative publicity together, the way Hyde and Lily would.

The bus finally pulled into the first station in Denver. She unloaded, clutching her purse. Walking through the terminal, she exited and stopped on the front sidewalk, pulling out her phone to get an Uber coming. The Uber driver confirmed quickly and she got a message to meet him in the south parking lot.

Walking over there, she glanced around and saw no one but empty cars. She felt so alone and she missed Mack. Why had she left him?

She heard from behind her, "Sariah."

She spun and her legs barely supported her. "Tyler?"

He looked polished and handsome as ever in a black suit with his dark hair slicked back from his face. He had a very handsome face, but he was a snake underneath. Two-timing her and Denise, and deserting Sariah to the negative publicity after everything went south. Not that she would've wanted him once she found out about him cheating on both of them, but he'd turned tail and run before she could tell him where to go. He'd be perfect for the political career he was hoping to achieve.

"What are you doing here?" she asked, leaning against a nearby bench.

He approached her slowly, staring at her. "I saw the media, about you and Mack Quinn."

"So now that I'm good enough for an NFL player I'm good enough for the future politician?"

His dark eyes flashed at her. "Mack Quinn isn't the right one for you, I am."

"Mack Quinn is one of the best men I know." She jutted her chin out, knowing that was true. She wished she was back in that hotel room with Mack. She'd gone over the edge this morning when those pictures came out and let her fears and trust issues mess up her thought process, but it was so clear now. Maybe she'd have to deal with some media exposure with Mack, but being loved by him was worth it. "And he doesn't have a crazy girlfriend whose brothers tortured me and lied to the world about me."

Tyler came into her space. Sariah stood her ground, not willing to back down to him at all.

"Are you ever going to forgive me for something I didn't do?"

"Two-timing Denise and I is something you did, Tyler."

"You *have* to forgive me. You know how crazy Denise was, the lies she spun. I was terrified of her so I lied to her that I loved her, but it was you I loved. Only you. You can't hold her lies and psycho twisting of life against me."

"I can hold a lot against you." Sariah blinked up at him. "Why do you even care? It's been years and you've never so much as texted me." She hated the way that had come out, as if she wanted him to text her.

"I've always cared. I've never stopped loving you."

"Please." Sariah laughed harshly then she pulled the hair away from the right side of her neck, exposing her neck and deformed ear. Tyler visibly cringed but he didn't back away. "You have to love all of a person, Tyler, and even without the Denise night-mare and your lies, you were always incapable of loving all of me." Mack wasn't. Mack had embraced her scars and would never ask her to cover them up. She wished he would've told her immediately he'd seen the pictures, but she understood why he was reluctant to, and he was right that she should've trusted him if she wanted to prove him trustworthy. He truly loved every part of her. Visions of him gently kissing her scars and then the way he'd taken her coverup off made her tremble. He thought she was beautiful and wanted her to share her beauty with the world. The contrast between him and Tyler was so stark she couldn't believe she'd allowed herself to hurt for so long and shut herself off from healthy relationships because of this snake of a man.

Tyler studied her. "Give me another chance, Sariah."

She rolled her eyes. "Get out of my face." Walking away from him, she clicked on the Uber app to see how close the driver was. She wanted away from this lonely parking lot, and especially from Tyler.

Tyler ripped the phone from her hand, dropping it on the cement.

"Hey," Sariah yelled, bending to pick it up.

Tyler grabbed her around the waist and began dragging her around cars.

"Let go," Sariah screamed, hitting at his arm and fighting to free herself.

"Calm down. I just want to talk to you alone."

"I'm done talking with you," she yelled back at him.

"Let her go." The voice was soothing and familiar. Sariah felt weak when she saw Mack standing in their path. His blond hair was tousled, his blue eyes determined, and his muscular frame looked bigger and more intimidating than ever. Sariah's heart leapt. He'd come for her, even after she'd treated him so horribly. Oh, how she loved him.

"Back off, Quinn," Tyler snarled.

Mack moved so quick, Tyler didn't even get his hands up. Mack grabbed Tyler's arm, wrenched him away from Sariah, and threw him to the ground. Tyler screeched and put up his hands. "Don't hit me."

"Don't ever touch her again." Mack towered over him.

Seconds ticked by and Tyler must've realized Mack wasn't going to hit him. He glared up at him. "I'll sue you and turn you into the police for assault."

Mack's eyebrows went up. "Really? I think Sariah's assault and attempted rape suit will take precedence over yours."

"I wasn't going to hurt her," he whined.

"Tell it to the judge. Your political career is over."

Tyler cowered before him. "I promise I'd never hurt her." He looked to Sariah. "Don't turn me in, please. I just wanted to love you."

"Never come near me again and maybe I won't press criminal charges, but Mack and I will both be telling the media all about what a loser you are." Sariah folded her arms across her chest.

She wouldn't mind Tyler serving time but she definitely wanted to make sure this man never represented her state in public office. She glanced up at Mack. With him by her side she could help spread the truth.

Sariah stared down at Tyler. It was just too coincidental that he had found her now. "Did you pay someone to follow me and take pictures of us the past two days?" she asked.

Tyler's eyes widened with fear, finally he admitted, "You haven't dated anyone since me so I thought someday we would be together again. When I heard you were dating Mack Quinn, and saw the pictures of you at Lily's wedding, I knew I had to get you back."

"You have no chance of ever getting me back," she said. "Go away and know that your political career is over."

"No," Tyler protested. "You wouldn't do that to me, Sariah. You have to still care for me."

Mack bent down closer to him. "The lady asked you to go away. Unless you want your nose broken, I suggest you leave ... now."

Tyler's face crumpled. He nodded and scrambled away from them in an awkward crabwalk like the insect he was, before jumping to his feet and running toward the bus station.

Mack turned to Sariah. "Are you okay?"

Sariah shook her head, tears pricking at her eyes.

Mack stepped closer to her. "Did he hurt you?" He glanced at where Tyler had disappeared, as if he would go after him and truly smash his nose for hurting Sariah.

"No." Sariah wrapped her palms around Mack's face and turned him back to look at her. "But I hurt you."

Mack's blue gaze softened. "I understand why you did."

"Sorry I overreacted."

"It's okay. And I might even recover ... if you promise never to leave me again."

Sariah's shoulders relaxed and she felt all lit up inside. Mack was here. They were back to their teasing. He was her hero.

"I might be able to promise that," she said, "If you can tell me you forgive me, and kiss me until I forget what state I was born in."

"That's easy. I'll always forgive you and kissing you is my favorite thing to do."

"Well then, get busy." Sariah grinned.

Mack laughed and wrapped his arms around her back, tugging her against him. Sariah arched up to meet him. His lips met hers and she was filled with love and acceptance.

Mack pulled back and traced his fingers along both sides of her neck, pushing her long hair further back from her face. She trembled under his touch. "I like your hair this way," he said.

The last vestiges of horror from seeing Tyler and feeling like she wasn't worthy of Mack disappeared. She could trust Mack and knew he'd embrace every part of her. "Do you now?"

He nodded. "I like all of you, in every way."

"Well, that's good because I love every bit of you too." She looked him over. "Lots to love."

"That's right." He grinned and softly kissed her again. "I love you back."

No more words were needed as Mack lifted her off the ground and proceeded to kiss her until she was certain that he loved all of her.

CHAPTER TWENTY-ONE

"**Y**ou ready for this?" Mack asked, squeezing her hand.

"Bring it on." Sariah winked at him, straightening her shoulders and pushing her hair behind her right ear. She'd broken the nervous habit of pulling it forward. The empowerment of loving herself was entwined in the beauty of how Mack loved her.

Mack looked devastatingly handsome in a navy-blue suit. She was wearing a sleeveless floral dress that showed off her shoulders and neck and hit just below her knees. Instead of feeling exposed and awkward, she felt pretty and light, but she always felt that way with Mack by her side.

Scarlett Lily approached them, having just finished her segment. She'd alluded to finding the love of her life and losing him as she talked about her new film. Sariah wondered if it was Griff, but wasn't sure how to ask.

"Are you on next?" Scarlett asked.

Mack shook the actress' hand. "Yes, ma'am. This is my fiancée, Sariah Udy."

Sariah also shook her hand. "It's fabulous to meet you. I love your shows."

"Thank you. So, you're one of the smart women who snagged a Quinn boy."

"Lucky women," Sariah corrected. She tilted her head. "I hear you're going to whip Griff into line for us."

Scarlett gave a chortled laugh as Mack threw back his head and roared with laughter. "Nobody could whip Griff into line," Mack said.

"I'm afraid he's right." Scarlett smiled, but it was strained. Her clear green eyes looked so sad Sariah couldn't help but hug her.

"Are you okay?" Sariah asked, wondering if her angst was related to her disappearance a few months ago. She'd avoided those questions in her interview pretty well.

Scarlett shook her head. "No, but I'm happy for you two."

Before Sariah could question her about whatever was going on, someone prompted from the side, "You're on."

"I hope we see you again," Sariah said to Scarlett.

"Me too." Scarlett waved.

Mack lifted his chin to Scarlett and escorted Sariah onto the stage. The lights were bright and the crowd loud as they cheered them on stage. Nerves had her stomach rolling. She had to fight against the urge to wrap her hair around her neck. Mack holding her hand and being by her side was the only thing that gave her strength to keep walking forward.

The host, Jessie, greeted them with air kisses and they took their seats.

"Now, we'll get to this lovely mass of muscles and his stats in a minute, but we want to hear about you, Sariah. You have a message you'd like to share with girls around the world?"

"Yes."

Mack squeezed her hand, giving her that smile that said she was the most beautiful woman in the world to him.

"You see, I used to think my scars were a deformity, but then I met the most amazing man and he taught me ..." She had to swallow past the lump in her throat. "That I'm beautiful, not in spite of, but because of my scars. The hard things we go through in life give us character, and if we can keep on smiling through the pain, we'll come out more beautiful on the other side."

The audience went crazy, clapping, screaming how beautiful she was. Sariah waited until they quieted and then she tried to explain better, "Every woman is a unique beauty. Don't compare yourself or concentrate on what isn't perfect about you. Shine with your own beauty."

The audience freaked out again, but Sariah was too busy staring at Mack. He tugged her close and kissed her, which made the audience go even more nuts.

"I love you," he whispered against her lips.

"Thanks for that."

He laughed, and ignoring the talk show host trying to question them, kissed her again.

Don't miss the rest of the Quinn family series:

1. The Devoted Groom: Texas Titan Romances - Ryder Quinn

2. The Conflicted Warrior: Sutton's Security Romances - Kaleb Quinn

3. The Gentle Patriot: Georgia Patriots Romances - Mack Quinn

4. The Tough Warrior: Navy SEAL Romances - Griff Quinn (Coming March 7)

AUTHOR'S NOTE

Twelve years ago I amputated three of my fingers with a lawn-mower. I was, of course, daydreaming up a story and stuck my fingers right into the blade. My poor mom and husband!

I thought I'd always feel awkward and embarrassed of my deformed fingers, but the love of my husband and help from above made me realize that I am loved and accepted no matter what happens to my exterior. I pray every one of us can realize that we may not appear perfect but we are beautiful in our one way, each of us has unique talents, and we can bless lives by focusing outside ourselves.

Much love,

Cami

ABOUT THE AUTHOR

Cami is a part-time author, part-time exercise consultant, part-time housekeeper, full-time wife, and overtime mother of four adorable boys. Sleep and relaxation are fond memories. She's never been happier.

Join Cami's VIP list to find out about special deals, giveaways and new releases and receive a free copy of *Rescued by Love: Park City Firefighter Romance* by clicking here.

Read on for a short excerpt of Sariah's sister, Lily's story in *The Loyal Patriot*.

cami@camichecketts.com
www.camichecketts.com

EXCERPT - THE LOYAL PATRIOT

Lily stepped into the office all the way and the man turned to face her. Lily's jaw dropped. Anybody with any kind of electronic device would recognize that good-looking face. "You're ..." She caught a breath. "Holy Toledo, you're Hyde Metcalf!"

He smiled, and she honestly wanted to swoon right then and there. "'Holy Toledo'?" he repeated.

She blushed.

On camera, Hyde Metcalf always had half a smile on his face, like he knew a joke everybody wanted to be privy to. But when he really smiled, wow, it was a good one. She didn't have as much insight as she wanted to about his personal life because she tried diligently not to become obsessive about him, but she knew he had an African American father who'd also played pro football back in his day and a beautiful blonde mother. He was the perfect blend of his parents. His eyes were dark and framed with long lashes, and his face was just nice—the right amount of manly lines with enough softness to make him real.

Just because she didn't allow herself to Google his personal life any more than once a week, or read every article put out by the gossip magazines about him, didn't mean she didn't know his every stat, watch his games faithfully, or follow him on Twitter, Instagram, Facebook ... really, wherever he had an account. Okay, truth be told, she was a geeky football fan and she was pathetically star-struck by Hyde Metcalf.

Her hands were trembling with nervous excitement, and she wasn't sure what her face was doing. She wanted to touch him and make sure he was real.

"And I hear you're Lily Udy," Hyde said, extending his hand to shake hers.

"The one and only." Lily gave him a firm handshake, liking the size of his hands. Of course they had to be big to snatch the ball out of the air like he did. Oh my goodness, he was real and he was standing right in front of her. She wanted to jump up and down, take a selfie with him, and call her brothers to tell them how amazing this was—she was meeting Hyde Metcalf and he knew *her* name. Her youngest brother, Josh, would go completely berserk.

"Malee is telling me you're the best sports-specific trainer in Golden," he said.

Lily cocked her head and tried to appear confident, though he could probably see the pulse in her neck jumping. "Maybe in the state of Colorado."

He chuckled. "Oh, I like confidence. This is the girl I need."

Need for what? Because she was totally up for whatever he needed. *Lily!* Her mother's voice in her head told her not to be infatuated with him just because the guy was a big-time football star. But come on, she loved him. Well, not *loved him,* loved him, but he was the best wide receiver to play the game. He had 1871 receiving yards last year. Plus, he was always just doing cool things. He'd coordinated an event to raise money for juvenile diabetes research and—from the video footage she'd seen—spent time with many of the children one on one. He'd helped a single mom with the medical bills for her daughter's cancer. He'd brought a young boy with spina bifida down on the field and had him throw in the game ball. The media captured all of it, and she knew famous people had a hard time hiding nowadays.

Okay, so maybe she Googled Hyde more often than once a week and knew a few things about his personal life. Not only was he unreal cool; he'd also grown up right here in Golden, only twenty minutes from her own hometown of Georgetown. It wasn't unusual that she felt such a connection to him.

"Hyde wanted to meet you before we signed the contract," Malee said.

"Contract?" *Oh my, calm down, heart. Hyde Metcalf is looking at me and smiling!*

"You probably heard about the pneumonia?" Hyde asked.

"Follow you on Twitter," she admitted.

"Nice. I like a girl who's informed." He folded those beautiful arms across his chest. Yum, what she wouldn't do to work with biceps like that, or touch them. Touching them would be a little creepy, though, right?

"I've recently been cleared to return to physical activity," Hyde was saying, and she tried to keep up as her head swam with visions of touching his biceps, "and I've got two months until practice starts full bore for the season. I'd like you to train me."

Lily had to grab on to a nearby chair.

Find *The Loyal Patriot* here.

ALSO BY CAMI CHECKETTS

Quinn Family Romance

The Devoted Groom

The Conflicted Warrior

The Gentle Patriot

Hawk Brothers Romance

The Determined Groom

The Stealth Warrior

Her Billionaire Boss Fake Fiance

Risking it All

Navy Seal Romance

The Protective Warrior

The Captivating Warrior

The Stealth Warrior

Texas Titan Romance

The Fearless Groom

The Trustworthy Groom

The Beastly Groom

The Irresistible Groom

The Determined Groom

The Devoted Groom

Billionaire Beach Romance

Caribbean Rescue

Cozumel Escape

Cancun Getaway

Trusting the Billionaire

How to Kiss a Billionaire

Onboard for Love

Shadows in the Curtain

Billionaire Bride Pact Romance

The Resilient One

The Feisty One

The Independent One

The Protective One

The Faithful One

The Daring One

Park City Firefighter Romance

Rescued by Love

Reluctant Rescue

Stone Cold Sparks

Snowed-In for Christmas

Echo Ridge Romance

Christmas Makeover

Last of the Gentlemen

My Best Man's Wedding

Change of Plans

Counterfeit Date

Snow Valley

Full Court Devotion: Christmas in Snow Valley

A Touch of Love: Summer in Snow Valley

Running from the Cowboy: Spring in Snow Valley

Light in Your Eyes: Winter in Snow Valley

Romancing the Singer: Return to Snow Valley

Fighting for Love: Return to Snow Valley

Other Books by Cami

Seeking Mr. Debonair: Jane Austen Pact

Seeking Mr. Dependable: Jane Austen Pact

Saving Sycamore Bay

How to Design Love

Oh, Come On, Be Faithful

Protect This

Blog This

Redeem This

The Broken Path

Dead Running

Dying to Run

Fourth of July

Love & Loss

Love & Lies

Cami's Collections

Cami's Military Collection

Billionaire Beach Romance Collection

Made in the USA
Monee, IL
19 March 2020

23519650R00108